WHERE TWO HEARTS MEET

Two Sweet Something Teashop Novellas

TEA FOR TWO

and

WHEREVER LOVE TAKES US

By
Carrie Turansky

TABLE OF CONTENTS

TEA FOR TWO

WHEREVER LOVE TAKES US

DEDICATION

To my daughters Melissa, Elizabeth, Megan,
Melinda, and Galan.

You are each a joy and blessing beyond compare . . .
so beautiful and special to me.
I love you!

"Love keeps no record of wrongs . . .
It always protects, always trusts, always hopes,
always perseveres."

1 CORINTHIANS 13:5,7

TEA FOR TWO

By Carrie Turansky

Chapter One

The bell over the front door of Sweet Something Teashop jingled, and the mailman stepped inside. A brisk March breeze followed him and swept through the shop, ruffling the white lace curtains at the front windows. He pushed the heavy oak and glass door closed, making the bell ring again.

Allison Bennett, co-owner of the shop, walked up front and greeted him with a smile. "Afternoon, Howard."

He nodded and handed her the small stack of mail. "Here you go."

"Thanks. Can I get you a hot cup of tea or coffee?"

"Not today. This weather has me behind schedule." He adjusted the plaid wool scarf around his neck and frowned toward the window. "I gotta keep moving."

"You sure? You look like you need to warm up."

He shook his head. "Thanks. I'll be all right."

"Okay. We'll see you tomorrow." She watched him duck

out the door, trudge past deep piles of slushy snow lining Nassau Street, and step into Princeton Interiors next door. Leaning closer to the front door's cool glass, she glanced up at the gray, brooding sky, and then down the empty sidewalk toward Princeton University. This morning she'd read an article in the *Princeton Packet* calling this the worst winter in thirty years. She sighed and shook her head. No doubt about that. Foot traffic along Princeton's historic Nassau Street had almost disappeared, taking most of her customers with it.

A dizzy, sick feeling washed over her as she thought of all she'd invested in her business over the last twelve months. If the weather didn't warm up soon, they could be in big trouble, maybe even be forced to close Sweet Something permanently.

She closed her eyes, trying to still her churning thoughts. *Please, Lord, help us get through these next few weeks. Send us an early spring.* She looked out the window again, imagining all the shoppers and business people who would stroll down the street and in the door for lunch or afternoon tea once the temperature rose and the sun came out. They'd come again. She had to believe it. Not just for herself, but for her sister's sake.

"Was that the mailman?" Tessa Malone, Allison's older sister, wiped her hands on a tea towel and glanced toward the front door. Short dark hair framed her pleasant face with a wispy fringe, and her cheeks glowed from working in the warm kitchen. Pretty green and gold beads dangled from her ears. She crossed from the antique desk that served as a hostess podium and stepped down into the gift shop area to meet Allison.

Allison shifted her gaze to the mail in her hand. "Yes.

Hopefully he didn't bring us any more bills."

Tessa's dark eyebrows dipped. "Better check and see."

Allison leafed through the pile, flipping past a color-ful grocery circular from McCaffery's Market and a coupon for a free session at Princeton Biofeedback Center. On the bottom of the pile, a plain white envelope with a neatly printed address caught her attention.

"I hope it's not one of those fund-raising letters from Princeton Hospital." Tessa pointed at Allison. "Don't even think about giving them any money right now."

Allison let Tessa's words pass without comment. She knew her sister's tendency to mother her came from their twelve-year age difference and close sister-bond. They shared management of the teashop, and though most of the financial investment came from Allison, Tessa faith-fully oversaw the baking and food preparation.

Allison slid her finger under the edge of the envelope and tore it open. Peeking in, she caught a glimpse of a ca-shier's check. "Oh my goodness. Look!" She pulled it out with a trembling hand.

Tessa leaned closer and scanned the check's inscrip-tion. Her dark eyes bulged, and she snatched the check from Allison. "Three thousand five hundred dollars! Look at the memo line: *FOR ALLISON AND SWEET SOMETHING*" She stared at Allison. "It's just like the other one."

Allison nodded, recalling the cashier's check for five thousand dollars she had received shortly before she opened the teashop on Valentine's Day a little over a year ago. "I can't believe this. Who would send me this much money?"

"I don't know. Maybe someone heard were having fi-nancial problems."

"I haven't told anyone. Have you?"

Tessa shook her head. "And I'm sure Matt wouldn't say anything. He's a stickler about ethical things like that."

Allison nodded. She trusted her brother-in-law completely. He was an experienced CPA and handled all the finances for Sweet Something. "I know we really need this, but it's a little spooky. How would someone know how much we need to cover the rest of this week's payroll and the increase in our rent?"

"They must have a direct line to *You Know Who* upstairs." Tessa lifted her gaze toward the ceiling, and she wasn't talking about the architect who rented the office above the teashop.

Goose bumps raced down Allison's arms. "Right. But I'd still like to know who He used to send it."

Tessa's eyes lit up, and she grinned. "I bet it's Peter."

Allison pulled back and wrinkled her nose. "No, it couldn't be."

"Why not? He has the money, and you know he's interested in you. He's here practically every day."

Allison couldn't imagine Peter Hillinger, the owner of Princeton Interiors, giving money to anyone anonymously. It wasn't his style. He wore perfectly tailored clothes from the best stores in Princeton and drove a new black BMW. And Peter never missed an opportunity to mention his successful business, even though he'd inherited it from his father less than three years ago.

"It would be easy for him to see how slow things have been."

Allison shook her head. "I don't think Peter would do something like this."

"Well, he certainly could if he wanted to." Tessa pursed

her lips and seemed offended that Allison didn't agree.

Allison glanced at the check again, remembering Peter's thoughtful comments about the teashop, his interest in her artwork, and his new habit of attending church with her. He seemed sincere. Maybe she was being too judgmental. Whoever had sent the check was very generous and most likely listening to the Lord. How else could he know their need?

"I suppose it could be Peter." Allison chewed her lower lip as she considered the idea. "But I got the first check over a year ago at church through Pastor Tom, and Peter didn't start coming to church with us until we invited him last fall."

"Okay, so Peter might not have given you the first check, but this one has to be from him. Who else could it be?"

Allison shrugged. "I don't know."

Tessa grinned. "I think you should say yes next time he asks for a date."

Allison's stomach tensed. She turned away and tucked the check back in the envelope. "He hasn't asked me out since I turned him down for Valentine's Day."

"All he needs is a little encouragement."

"But it doesn't seem fair to encourage him. We're just friends. That's all I—"

"Friendship is a great place to start. Spend more time with him. Give it a chance." Tessa touched Allison's cheek, a look of concern in her eyes. "There's someone special out there for you. I know it. But you have to be willing to let go of the past, open up your heart, and try again."

Tears misted Allison's eyes. Of course her sister was right. She needed to bury those painful memories once and for all. Six years was long enough to wait for someone who was never coming back.

* * * *

The tantalizing scent of freshly baked blackberry pie drifted toward Tyler Lawrence as he stepped into the warmth of Sweet Something Teashop. Rubbing his hands together to warm them, he glanced around the cozy interior.

Antique sideboards and small tables displayed interesting collections of china teapots, cups, and saucers. Whimsical birdhouses and small table lamps with painted shades sat on the shelves between the front windows. Little packages of specialty teas in cellophane bags tied with pink ribbons stood in neat rows ready for purchase. He hadn't expected Sweet Something to have a gift shop as well as a tearoom. But, knowing Allie's love for art and her romantic, creative style, it made sense.

The shop's feminine ambiance announced its owner as clearly as if her name had been painted on the WELCOME sign. He glanced into the quiet tearoom and saw only two tables occupied.

Allie stepped down into the gift shop and past a large armoire filled with round hatboxes, dried flowers, and antique crystal dishes. Her gaze connected with his, and recognition flashed in her eyes.

Tyler smiled. "Hi, Allie." She looked just as beautiful as she had the day he'd left Princeton six years ago. She'd cut her rich caramel-colored hair in a new style that brushed her shoulders. A few soft lines at the corners of her eyes testified to the passing years, but those were the only hints

12

of change he noticed.

She stared at him, questions shimmering in her dark blue eyes.

"I heard about your shop. I thought I'd stop in and say hello."

She darted a glance over her shoulder and then back at him. "I'll get you a menu." She turned and walked toward the tearoom, leaving a faint flowery fragrance in her wake. She wore a mocha-colored blouse with soft flowing ruffles at her neck and wrists, and a long, slim black skirt. He spotted brown leather boots through the slit in her skirt as she stepped up into the tearoom.

He followed, sending off a prayer for grace. He didn't deserve it, but over the past two years, he'd learned God's grace and forgiveness could cover a multitude of sins. He needed both of those from Allie as well.

In all those years he'd seen her only once—a little over a year ago on Christmas Eve at church. The scene flashed through his mind as he crossed the tearoom. He had returned to Princeton to spend the holidays with his mother for the first time in five years. After the service, he'd unexpectedly bumped into Allie and fumbled a lame apology, saying something about being sorry he hadn't kept in touch. Of course that was true, but it didn't even begin to address the real issues between them. It certainly didn't ease his guilt or erase the pain in her eyes.

Allie led him to a small table for two in the corner.

He sat down and smiled up at her.

She averted her eyes and handed him a menu printed on light pink paper. "We have several choices for lunch, or our tea and dessert menu is on the back. Can I get you something to drink?"

13

Her cool formality cut him to the heart. "Can you sit down for a few minutes?"

"No, I'm busy," she said, without missing a beat.

"It doesn't look like you have too many customers right now. Couldn't you take a break? I'd like to hear more about Sweet Something. How long have you been open?" Of course he knew the answer to that question, but he hoped it would draw her into a conversation.

Her gaze dropped to the menu in his hand. "All right, but let me take your order first."

"I'd like tea and something sweet. What do you recommend?" She hesitated a moment. "The apple cinnamon scones are popular, or if you'd like something more substantial, you could try the blackberry cobbler or lemon lush. They're in the glass case over there if you'd like to take a look." Allie seemed to relax a little as she described the dessert choices.

"What's your favorite?" he asked, keeping his tone light.

"They're all good. Tessa does our baking."

"Your sister works here with you?"

"Yes." Allie smoothed her hand down her skirt.

"That's great. How's she doing?" He hoped this question might transition the conversation to a more personal level.

"Her husband's business failed a couple years ago. They lost their house and most of their savings." She spoke in an even tone, but her eyes revealed her concern.

"I'm sorry. That sounds like a tough situation."

"Matt and Tessa are trying to get back on their feet. That's why we opened Sweet Something." Allie's face flushed, and she bit her lip.

Tyler realized he'd better shift the direction of the conversation. "I like the way you've decorated the shop." He hesitated, glancing around the almost empty room again. "How's business?"

"We're doing all right."

"Really?"

Her bravado melted. She lowered her gaze, frowning slightly. "Actually, the weather has hurt us. There's not much parking on the street, and the closest public lot is four blocks away. Most people don't want to hike that far on slushy sidewalks when it's freezing." A look of tired resignation filled her face.

"Maybe I can help."

She cocked her head, looking doubtful. "What do you mean?"

"Please, sit down. Let's talk."

She stood a moment more, then finally took the seat on the opposite side of the table.

"I have a new job with an ad agency here in Princeton. Maybe I could do a little promotional work for you. You know, raise your visibility and get some more customers coming through the door."

Her face flushed. "We've already used all our advertising budget for this year."

"Oh, I wouldn't charge you. I'd do it on my own time."

She sat back, shaking her head slightly. "I couldn't let you do that."

"Come on, Allie." He leaned toward her, his excitement growing. "I could create a logo, a new sign, and a menu. I could check out your local advertising options and see what's available. It won't cost you a penny, I promise." Confidence flowed through him. With his help, her business could flourish no matter what the weather sent her way.

Suspicion clouded her eyes. "Why would you do that for me?"

A painful realization twisted through him. She didn't trust him or his motives. Why should she? She only knew him as the man he'd been six years ago, when he'd left town with no explanation and broken every promise he'd made to her.

"I just want to help you." He pulled in a ragged breath, struggling to remember the apology he had so carefully crafted back at his office. But it evaporated like a frosty breath on a winter day.

She stared at him, her expression unreadable, as though she'd constructed a wall around herself.

"Look, I know I messed up before, and you have no reason to trust me. But honestly, all I want to do is make up for what happened. We had something special, Allie. I'm sorry I let you go."

Her deep blue eyes flashed a warning, and her mouth firmed into a straight line. She rose from her chair and turned away.

Tyler stood. "Allie, wait. That's not what I wanted to say."

She spun around, and her piercing gaze nailed him to the spot. "I don't want your help with my business, and I'm not interested in discussing the past."

Regret swamped him. If he could only go back and change his foolish choices. But that was impossible. He'd already reaped a harvest of pain from those mistakes, but it looked like harvest season wasn't over yet.

He turned to go, but something made him look over his shoulder. Allie stood by the table, watching him, sorrow clouding her eyes. That gave him the courage to turn around and walk back toward her. "If you change your mind, I'd still like to help you get the word out about Sweet Something." He took his business card from his pocket and held it out to her.

A spark of some indefinable emotion flickered in her eyes. She reached out and accepted his card.

Chapter Two

Allison wiped the stainless-steel counter while visions of yesterday's confrontation with Tyler clouded her mind. The warmth of the teashop kitchen and slow pace of the afternoon lulled her into a dreamy fog.

Or had the air suddenly become strangely hazy?

She stopped to sniff, then spun toward the oven. Little blue-gray curls of smoke leaked out around the edges of the oven door. She gasped and lunged for a heavy-quilted oven mitt.

Tessa rushed in from the tearoom. "Something's burning!"

"I know!"

"Hurry, we don't want the smoke alarms to go off again." Tessa flipped on the overhead fan and unlocked the back window.

Allison jerked open the oven door. Clouds of smoke puffed into the room. Coughing, she grabbed the cookie sheet of scorched scones and crossed to the open window. In one swift motion, she flipped the cookie sheet and dumped the smoking triangles onto the brick walk out back. They looked more like smoking volcanic rocks than anything edible. Even the poor birds wouldn't be interested in that mess.

Allison moaned and tossed the cookie sheet into the deep stainless-steel sink. "I can't believe I did that twice in one day!"

"Me neither." Tessa flapped a blue-striped kitchen towel back and forth.

"I'm sorry. I should have set the timer."

The air began to clear, and Tessa hung the towel on a hook by the sink. "You've been distracted all morning. Does this have anything to do with Tyler stopping in yesterday?"

Allison scowled. "No!"

Tessa crossed her arms. "Come on. Admit it. You were thinking about him instead of keeping your eyes on those scones."

Allison pushed her hair back from her warm face. "Okay, I was. But you'd be distracted, too, if you'd heard what he said. I can't believe he thinks he can just walk back in here and have a friendly conversation after six years with no communication."

"You never heard from him that whole time?"

"No!" She faltered, remembering that wasn't exactly true. "Well, I did see him on Christmas Eve, a year ago." She fiddled with her watch clasp. Confusion swirled through her as she recalled his tender look and halting apology. She forced those thoughts away and focused on the painful end of their relationship six years ago. He'd made her believe he loved her. They'd even talked about getting married, but then he'd left without even saying good-bye. She still didn't know why. She sighed and rubbed her stinging eyes.

"I'm sorry." Tessa laid her hand on Allison's arm. "I didn't know it still bothered you."

"Neither did I, until yesterday." She steeled herself

against those painful memories. "He has a lot of nerve, waltzing in here and offering to do promotional work for Sweet Something."

"Wait a minute. He wants to do promotional work for us?"

"Yes. Can you believe it?" Allison tossed the oven mitt onto the counter. "He works for some ad agency and thought we might like some free advertising advice."

Tessa gasped. "He wouldn't charge us?" She grabbed Allison's arm. "Please tell me you said yes."

"Nooo!" Allison vigorously shook her head.

"And why not?"

"You remember what happened! Not only did he walk out on me, he dropped out of grad school, got arrested for DUI, and our friends said he was just a . . . player."

"A player?" Tessa leaned back against the counter.

"You know—a guy who goes from girl to girl, playing with their emotions, just looking for . . ." She lifted her eyebrows and sent her sister a meaningful glance.

"Oh . . . well, that was a long time ago."

Allison touched her heart. "It doesn't feel like it to me."

Tessa frowned, but only for a moment. Then her face brightened. "That was personal. This is business." She crossed her arms. "I hope you weren't rude to him. What did you say?"

"Well . . . I think I said I didn't want his help." She'd practically kicked him out of the shop, and his calm response totally stumped her. Where was the cocky, self-assured man who always had a quick comeback or persuasive excuse for everything?

Tessa groaned. "Allison, how could you? Call him right now, and tell him you've changed your mind."

"I can't do that!"

"Oh, yes you can. We need his help. And if you're worried about things getting uncomfortable, just insist on keeping it strictly business."

Conflicting thoughts tumbled through Allie's mind. Spending time with Tyler would be awkward. But wasn't keeping her business afloat worth dealing with a little emotional upheaval? Certainly she could set aside her personal feelings and deal with him on a professional level. After all, she was an experienced businesswoman now.

She looked up at Tessa. "You're right. I can do this." She reached into her apron pocket and pulled out his business card.

Tessa leaned closer. She read it and sucked in a quick breath. "He works for Kent & Sheldon?"

"Yes. What about it?"

"That's one of the most prestigious ad agencies in Princeton. I heard the CEO is a Christian. He gives a lot to charity, and his agency only works with companies who are ethical."

Allison studied the card. Why would Tyler choose to work for a company like Kent & Sheldon?

* * * *

Tyler raised the collar of his navy wool overcoat and tucked his small portfolio under his arm. He hopped a slushy puddle and crossed Nassau Street with the WALK signal. A bone-chilling breeze whistled around the edge of his collar and cuffs, but the sun had come out. The sidewalks were dry, making it a little less intimidating to walk around town.

21

The last forty-eight hours had been a mad dash of creativity as he'd followed up on Allie's surprise phone call. With permission from Ronald Sheldon, he'd taken time off to research teashops and come up with several creative ideas for Sweet Something.

He smiled, remembering Allie's comments. "I'm sorry I was so quick to dismiss your offer. I've talked it over with Tessa, and we'd appreciate any advertising advice you could give us."

In a businesslike tone, she reminded him that their budget might not allow them to implement his ideas right away, but she'd like to see what he had in mind. He assured her he could come up with several options for free or low-cost advertising, and he'd do the graphic design at no charge.

"Let me work on this for a couple of days," he told her. "I'll get back to you. Shall I call you at home?"

"Call me at the shop," she said quickly. "I appreciate your help, but this is strictly business. I'm not interested in anything else."

That had deflated him a little, but his goals were to help Allie's business become successful and try to make up for the past. Anything else between them was up to the Lord. He didn't intend to push or manipulate the situation, no matter how strongly the old attraction pulled him. Pure motives. Pure actions. That had to be his focus now.

Tyler slowed as he passed Princeton Interiors, the shop next door to Sweet Something. Warm light glowed on a dazzling array of expensive antique furniture, chandeliers, and unique home decor. One glance at the busy shop, and he could tell the owner did a brisk business.

He continued on and pulled open the door of Sweet

Something. As he stepped inside, he looked past the gift shop into the tearoom. Customers filled more than half the tables. Tyler smiled. That ought to raise Allie's spirits and give her business a boost.

Allie hurried down the steps, her gaze fixed on the group of three middle-aged women who had come in before him. He stepped back and watched her welcome and seat the women at a round table in the center of the room.

Today Allie wore a royal blue blouse, the same color as her eyes, and a dark print skirt with swirls of sable brown, olive green, and deep blue. A white apron edged with lace topped her outfit.

He looked for other servers, but saw only one young woman weaving between the tables, carrying a tray of dirty dishes toward the back of the shop. Two other tables nearby still needed to be cleared.

He stepped into Allie's line of vision. When their gazes connected, her smile faltered for a moment but then returned. She nodded and walked toward him.

He smiled. "Looks like business is improving."

"Yes, this is the best day we've had in quite a while." Her cheeks flushed a pretty pink, and she sent him a cautious glance. "I know I asked you to come at three thirty, but I don't think I can meet with you today. Tessa had to leave early to take her daughter to the orthodontist, and two of my servers called in sick."

"Sounds like you're in a bind."

"Kayla and I will be tired by six, but we'll make it." She glanced at the clock and pulled in a sharp breath. "I have a group of ten from the Princeton Historical Society coming at four, and I haven't rearranged the tables in the other room." The bell jingled, and two young college-age girls in faded jeans, heavy jackets, and knit hats came in the door. Allie hesitated, looking torn. "I'm sorry. I have to take care of them." She excused herself and seated the girls. The other server hurried past with a tray of three small teapots, cups, and saucers.

Tyler surveyed the scene a moment longer and made his decision. Slipping off his coat, he followed Allie across the room. "Where can I stash this?"

She turned to him, questions in her eyes. "I'm sorry. I really can't meet with you today."

"I know. That's why I'm going to help you."

"What?" Her blue eyes widened.

"I've never actually served tea before, but I can rearrange tables, seat people, or do whatever else you need."

She stared at him as though she couldn't quite believe he was serious.

"Allie, you're shorthanded, and I have the rest of the afternoon off. This sounds like the perfect solution."

"But you can't do that," she sputtered. "You're a . . . professional, not a waiter."

"True, but I'm also a friend who wants to see your business succeed."

Her expression softened. "You're serious?"

"Sure. Where do I get one of those aprons?" He gestured toward the lacey one she wore.

She laughed, and it was a beautiful sound, almost like the tinkling of delicate wind chimes. "All right. You're hired. Come with me, and I'll show you where you can hang your coat." She led the way into the kitchen.

A few minutes later he had taken off his suit jacket, rolled up his sleeves, and tied a more masculine version of Allie's apron around his waist. She led the way to a side room and quickly mapped out the new table arrangement. Then she laid out one place setting on a side table as an example and showed him where the dishes were kept. "I'll be back in a few minutes." She smiled at him over her shoulder, then returned to the tearoom and left him to his work

Kayla, Allie's only other server, swept in and dropped off a pile of fresh table linens. The young blond didn't look more than eighteen. She hung around and asked him several questions. He gave brief answers as he moved tables and covered them with tablecloths. She finally turned to leave the room, sending him a seductive smile. He turned away from her obvious invitation, thankful those old temptations didn't have as much pull as they used to. A few years ago it might have been more of a struggle, but he was committed to a new path now.

Setting the table took a little longer than he'd expected. He finally stood back and surveyed his work with a satisfied smile.

Allie walked in carrying two small teapots holding arrangements of fresh flowers. She stepped up beside him, her gaze searching the table. "This looks perfect." She set the flowers on the table and beamed him a dazzling smile. "Thank you, Tyler."

He pulled in a deep breath and felt like he could walk a mile in the cold with the memory of that smile to warm him. "What's next?"

"Oh, you don't have to do anything else. This was a huge help."

"Hey, I'm not leaving now. I signed on for the whole afternoon." He straightened a knife and spoon at one place setting. "When this group shows up, you're going to have your hands full. I can greet and seat your other customers. And if that doesn't keep me busy, I can clear tables."

Allie protested, but he insisted. Soon he was doing double duty as host and busboy, while Allie and Kayla took orders and delivered food and drinks. The afternoon passed swiftly, and before he knew it, the clock by the front door struck six, and Allie flipped the OPEN sign to CLOSED.

With a relieved sigh, she smiled and gestured toward the closest table. "Why don't we sit down and take a look at your designs?"

He reached to untie his apron. "I'm sorry. I'd love to show them to you, but I'm supposed to meet a client at the Nassau Inn for dinner." He glanced at his watch. He needed to hurry or he'd be late.

She bit her lip a moment, then lifted her gaze to meet his. "Are you busy after that?"

He could hardly hold back his smile. "No. I don't have anything else planned tonight."

Allie took a business card from the basket and wrote something on the back. "I live just a few blocks from Nassau Inn. Here's the address. Could you stop by after dinner?" Her hand trembled slightly as she passed him the card.

Suddenly, he realized how much it had cost her to give him the invitation. He smiled and nodded. "This dinner won't take long." He'd make sure it didn't.

"All right. I'll see you later then." She sent him a tentative smile.

His hopes soared.

Chapter Three

Allison hurried up the steps and unlocked her front door. Her Persian cat, Miss Priss, jumped down from the back of the couch to greet her.

"Hello, sweetie." She gave Miss Priss a quick pat on the head and kissed her cold nose; then she hurried into the bathroom to brush her hair upside down, wash her face, and dab on some makeup. She changed twice before she finally settled on dark brown slacks, a white turtleneck, and a dark brown sweater with a snowflake pattern across the front.

Glancing in the mirror, Allison plastered on a smile and tried to think positive. But those last fifteen pounds she always intended to lose remained firmly attached in all the wrong places. She tugged at the bottom edge of her sweater, wishing it were a little longer. Why hadn't she kept up her exercise routine this winter, or at least said no to all those desserts Tessa asked her to try?

Blowing out a resigned sigh, she turned and walked away from the mirror. It didn't matter. This was not a date. They were simply going to look over his designs and discuss promotional ideas for Sweet Something.

R-i-i-ight. She rolled her eyes and knew she hadn't even

fooled herself. She hurried into the kitchen and fixed a pot of coffee.

The doorbell rang. Her heart jumped. She hurried across the living room but then slowed and pulled in a deep breath. Lord, help me calm down and not act like a complete idiot. They were going to discuss business and that's all. Relaxing a little, she pulled open the front door and greeted Tyler.

He smiled, looking as handsome as ever, his face flushed from the cold and his brown eyes glowing. A few snowflakes melted in his light brown hair and dusted the shoulders of his navy blue coat. She invited him in. He took off his coat, suit jacket, and scarf, and she hung them in the closet.

"This is very nice." He looked around her living room with an appreciative glance. Tyler had always noticed color, texture, and style. She guessed it was part of his artistic nature. Allison liked that about him. He understood her need to use her creativity and be surrounded by beauty.

"How about some coffee?" she offered. "I just made a pot. Or I have tea or cocoa."

"Coffee sounds great. Thanks. It's freezing outside." He rubbed his hands together and followed her into the kitchen. He slowed and slipped his hands into his pockets as he studied the painting on the wall near her kitchen table.

The painting featured a cozy living room setting, with two red wingback chairs pulled up by a stone fireplace where a welcoming fire glowed. A round table set for dessert stood between the chairs. A sleepy gray cat sat curled up in one of the chairs, and an open Bible lay on the footstool by the other.

He leaned closer, looking as though he wanted to take in every detail of the painting. "This is an original, isn't it?"

"Yes, it is." She pulled two mugs from the cabinet.

"Who's the artist?"

Allison looked up and met Tyler's gaze. "I am."

"I thought so." He smiled at her for a brief moment then turned back to the painting. "Why no signature?"

"It's there, but when I had it framed, the mat covered it." She filled the mugs with steaming coffee and carried them over to the kitchen table.

He spun and looked at her with a glint of excitement in his eyes. "Do you have other paintings?"

She nodded, wondering why he was so interested. "I have two upstairs in my bedroom and probably a dozen or so stored in the hall closet."

He sent her a baffled look. "In the closet?"

"Yes. It's too expensive to have them all framed."

"You know, there's a huge market for paintings like this. I saw several artists advertising their limited-edition prints when I scanned some home-decorating magazines, looking for logo ideas for Sweet Something. None of those paintings were as good as yours. You should have prints made."

A warm glow spread through her. Tyler was also an artist, making his compliment even more meaningful. They'd met in an art class in college. He had chosen to focus on graphic design and advertising, while she had decided on fine art and teaching, but their love of art had been a common thread woven through their two-year relationship.

She glanced at her painting, considering his idea. "That would probably take a big investment of time and money, and I need to focus on the shop right now." She set the mugs on the table and offered him sugar and cream.

"Why don't I look into it for you?" Tyler stirred a spoonful of sugar into his coffee. "It might not cost as much as you think." She started to shake her head, but the hopeful look in his eyes stopped her. "I guess it wouldn't hurt."

"Great!" His smile spread wider. "I can see it now—original paintings and prints by Allison Bennett hanging in galleries all across the country. You'll become famous, and before we know it, that'll draw huge crowds to your teashop. That's probably the best promotional idea we could ever come up with."

She laughed. "Tyler, you always were a dreamer."

He took a sip and gazed at her over the rim of his mug. "I've always known you had a special gift." He nodded toward her artwork. "That painting proves it. It draws you in, makes you feel like you could step right into that room." He focused on the cozy scene. "You've invited a good friend over for the evening. You light the fire, put on the coffee, slice the pie, and get out your Bible so you can sit down and talk about what you've been learning."

She sent him a curious glance. "That's exactly what I had in mind." Most people who'd looked at the painting didn't even realize the open book on the footstool was a Bible. But Tyler had.

He nodded, looking pleased, and took another sip of coffee. "So, are you ready to take a look at my designs for Sweet Something?"

She agreed, picked up her cup, and led the way to the living room.

Tyler opened his portfolio and spread out his designs on the coffee table, then took a seat beside her on the couch. "I worked with several different concepts, but these three are the strongest. Of course we can always combine ideas and change things around."

Allison was suddenly very conscious of Tyler's nearness. His shoulder brushed against hers as he reached to pick up the first design, and the warm spicy scent of his aftershave tickled her nose. She clasped her hands and forced herself to focus.

Tyler explained how he came up with the logos. Then he showed her each one on menus, business cards, a new outdoor sign, a newspaper ad, even gift certificates and discount coupons. "So what do you think? Which do you like best?" Confidence and expectation glowed in his eyes. He seemed to have no doubt she'd like his work.

"They're all beautiful. I'm not sure how to choose one."

"Go with your feelings. Which one stands out to you?"

"Well . . . I guess I'd say this one." She pointed to the logo featuring a delicate teacup and a soft pink rose in full bloom. The swirling green type and soft pastel colors in the rose and cup looked sophisticated yet fresh and inviting—just the image she wanted to project.

"That's actually my favorite, too." He turned to her and smiled. His expression softened, and tenderness filled his eyes as his gaze traveled over her face and hair.

Allison felt certain he wasn't thinking about logo designs anymore. Her heartbeat sped up, and she held her breath, waiting to hear what he would say next.

The doorbell rang. Allison jumped as if someone had poked her with a sharp stick. "Sorry. Excuse me a minute. I'll see who that is." She crossed the living room, pulled opened the door, and stared in stunned silence.

"Hello, Allison." Peter Hillinger leaned forward and kissed her cheek.

How could she have forgotten she had a dinner date

with Peter? Her mind whirled back to the day she had received the anonymous check. Right after Tyler had walked out the door of her shop, Peter had come in. When he'd invited her out to dinner, she'd been so flustered she'd said yes without thinking it through or writing it down.

"May I come in?"

"Yes, of course . . . I'm sorry." She stepped back and darted a glance at Tyler. He stood and looked Peter over warily.

A slight frown creased Peter's high forehead when he saw Tyler. He sent Allison a questioning glance.

She forced a tight smile. "Peter, this is Tyler Lawrence. He's . . . an old friend, and he's offered to do some promotional work for the teashop." She turned to Tyler, her mind spinning as she tried to come up with an explanation. "This is Peter Hillinger. He owns Princeton Interiors, the shop next to ours."

The two men shook hands, a challenge obvious in both their eyes.

Peter turned back to Allison. "Our dinner reservations are for eight o'clock, but I think they'll hold them for a few minutes if you'd like to change."

She glanced down at her outfit. "Oh . . . yes, I guess I should." She turned to Tyler, wishing she could explain. "I'm sorry. It looks like we'll have to finish this another time."

"No problem. I'll call you." He smiled, but disappointment clouded his eyes. At least she hoped it was disappointment and not irritation because she'd cut their evening short.

* * * *

Tyler watched Allie walk down the hall and slip into the first room on the right. Regret burned in his throat. There would be no more opportunity to talk to her tonight.

He felt Peter's haughty glare even before he turned to face him. Peter wore an expensive-looking black wool overcoat, white silk scarf, and leather gloves. Tyler had spent less than two minutes with the man, but that was long enough to know he didn't like him. His puffed-up attitude was bad enough, but the way he'd kissed Allie and walked into her house like he owned it, bothered him even more.

"So you're an old friend of Allison's?" Peter pulled off his gloves.

"Yes, we've known each other since college."

"That's funny." Peter sent him a slight smile. "I don't remember her ever mentioning you."

Those words cut deeply, and it took him a moment to recover. "Allie and I lost touch for a few years, but I'm back in Princeton now."

Peter glanced at the designs on the table. He lifted his brows for a brief moment, looking impressed, then glanced back at Tyler. "Interesting. But I'm not sure Allison needs any of this."

"I suppose that's up to her, isn't it?" Tyler gathered up his artwork, slid them back into his portfolio, and closed the flap.

"I appreciate your wanting to help Allison with her business, but I hope that's all you have in mind."

Tyler gripped the handles of the portfolio, wishing he could knock the pompous expression off Peter's face. A verse he had memorized flew to the front of his thoughts. *A foolish man gives full vent to his anger, but a wise man keeps himself under control.* He walked away from Peter and grabbed his jacket and coat from the closet.

Peter followed as though he were the host and intended to show Tyler out the door. "Allison has been through a lot over the past year, helping her sister through everything that's happened, and she's had a rather difficult time getting her business up and running. I've been there for her every step of the way." He narrowed his steel gray eyes, looking as though he wanted to make sure Tyler understood the message behind his words. "We've grown very close. I wouldn't want anyone to hurt her." Tyler squared his shoulders and locked gazes with Peter. "Neither would I." He turned and walked out the door.

* * * *

"You invited him over to your house?" Tessa turned from brushing crumbs off one of the tearoom tables and stared at Allison.

"Well, he wanted to show me his design ideas." Allison straightened the stack of menus, trying to ignore the disapproval in her sister's eyes.

"Right, I'm sure he had all kinds of designs he wanted to show you."

"Tessa, nothing happened! We had coffee and looked at his promotional plans for about twenty minutes. Then Peter came to pick me up for dinner." That thought left her feeling like a deflated balloon. After she'd changed and walked back into the living room, Peter was the only one waiting for her.

"So how was your date with Peter?"

"We went to Lambertville Station. The food was good. There was a jazz trio playing."

"So things are progressing?"

"I suppose. Peter's just so . . ." She squinted, trying to come up with the right word.

"Mature, confident, wealthy?"

Allison rolled her eyes. "Too bad you're already married. You could date him!"

"We're not talking about me. Were talking about you and Peter."

"I know." Confusion swirled through Allison. "I like him. He's thoughtful and interesting, but there's something missing. It's like I have to try too hard with him. And I just don't feel a connection with him like I do with Ty. . ." She swallowed the rest of her sentence and turned to push in the chairs at the nearest table.

"You're not thinking about dating Tyler again, are you?" Tessa tapped her nails on the oak desk they used as a hostess podium.

"I didn't say that."

"Good. Remember what happened last time. He left town and broke your heart."

She winced at her sister's words. "I know. You don't have to remind me."

"Sorry." Tessa softened her tone. "I just don't want you to get hurt again."

"Don't worry. I won't let Tyler talk me into anything more than a business relationship." But as Allison turned and glanced across the quiet teashop, she remembered how Tyler had spent the previous afternoon greeting customers and clearing tables for her. He seemed different somehow—still charming and persuasive as ever, but there was a softening, a gentleness about him that was new . . . and very attractive.

35

"Allison?" Tessa tapped her on the shoulder. "Did you hear what I said?"

"No. Sorry, guess I was daydreaming."

"About Peter or Tyler?"

"Tessa, stop! I am not interested in Tyler." Allison huffed and strode toward the kitchen.

* * * *

Four days was long enough to wait. Allison slipped Tyler's business card from her apron pocket and picked up the phone. She glanced at the clock by the front door, hoping she could make the call and connect with Tyler before her sister returned from the bank. The shop didn't open until eleven, so she didn't need to worry about taking care of customers for at least another hour. She quickly punched in his number and whispered a prayer. On the third ring the receptionist answered. Allison willed her voice to sound confident as she asked to speak to Tyler.

"I'm sorry, Mr. Lawrence is out of the office this morning. May I take a message?"

"Yes. Mr. Lawrence showed me some designs last Tuesday, but our meeting was interrupted. I've been expecting him to call so we could set up another meeting."

"I'm sure he meant to get back to you, but he's been sick for a few days."

Her heart jerked. "I hope it's nothing serious."

"I really couldn't say, but if you'd like to leave your name and number, I'll let him know you called."

Allison left the information and hung up the phone. She glanced out the teashop's front windows. Gray storm clouds gathered, and wind whistled in the eaves. Where was the promise of spring? She shivered and rubbed her arms.

Over the past week her financial troubles had become increasingly clear. The anonymous check had been a wonderful gift that carried them through early March, but unless she could bring in more customers soon, her business was doomed.

She closed her eyes. *Father, I can't live off my savings forever, and You know how much Tessa and Matt need the extra income. We have to start making a profit. I need Tyler's help for that, but I'm afraid I've botched things with him, and now he's sick.*

Little vines of worry wrapped around her heart as she considered the possibilities. How sick was he? Had he seen a doctor? Was anyone checking on him?

Chapter Four

Allison slipped the heavy basket over her arm and rang Tyler's doorbell. Her heartbeat surged in her ears as she strained to hear any sounds inside his apartment.

Nothing. She bit her lip and rang again. This plan had to work. Her only hope was to make amends with Tyler and convince him to follow through on his offer to do free promotional work for Sweet Something.

Finally, she heard a soft shuffle and the door swung open. Tyler looked out at her through red-rimmed, watery eyes. His baggy gray sweatpants and a wrinkled navy blue T-shirt made it look as though he had just crawled out of bed. He blinked at her. "Allie, what are you doing here?"

Heat rose in her cheeks, and she forced a smile. "I called your office, and they told me you were sick, so I thought I'd bring you some lunch."

"Wow, that's nice. Would you like to come in?" He stepped back and glanced over his shoulder. "Sorry, things are kind of a mess."

"You don't have to apologize. I can tell you've been sick."

He ran a hand over his bristly chin and sent her a sheepish grin. "I probably look worse than my apartment."

He looked adorable, but she quickly squelched that thought. "You look like a guy who needs to sit down and put his feet up." She pointed toward the dark brown leather couch. "Go on." Tyler obediently headed for the couch. He tossed his pillow to one end and straightened the blanket and sheet before he sat down. "So what's in the basket?" She set it on the coffee table next to a worn, brown leather Bible. That surprised her. Of course she knew Tyler had prayed and asked Christ into his heart when he was twenty-one. She'd been with him that night. But everything she'd heard about him since he'd left Princeton made her doubt his sincerity. If he was serious about his faith, how could he have been arrested for drinking and driving? And worse yet, how could he have a reputation for being involved in a string of broken relationships? Her stomach clenched at that thought.

Focusing on her basket, she folded back the blue tea towel. "I brought you some homemade chicken-noodle soup, blueberry muffins, applesauce, bottled water, tissues, and some cold and flu medication." She felt a little embarrassed by the overflowing collection she'd put together for him. But she needed him to get well as soon as possible.

He sent her an appreciative smile. "I haven't been able to eat much for a few days, but soup sounds great."

"Good. Why don't I warm some up for you?"

He glanced toward the kitchen. "I haven't cleaned up in there for a couple days."

"It's okay. You lie down and rest, and I'll be back with some hot soup in a couple minutes."

"Okay, thanks."

She picked up the basket and headed for the adjoining kitchen. Her steps slowed as she scanned the room. Dirty dishes and sticky pots and pans cluttered the counter and sink. Newspapers lay scattered on the small kitchen table, as well as a stack of unopened mail, two empty coffee cups, and a take-out bag from Mrs. Chow's Chinese Restaurant. She looked for a microwave, but didn't see one. So she checked the cabinet and found a pan, poured in the soup, and turned on the burner. She decided to rinse the dishes and load the dishwasher while she waited for the soup to warm. Glancing at the windowsill, she noticed a stack of 3 x 5 cards. Leaning closer, she saw a Bible reference written on the top card in Tyler's neat, all-cap handwriting. Surprise rippled through her.

"Are you finding everything you need?" Tyler called.

Allison jumped. "Yes, no problem."

"Sounds like more is happening in there than warming up the soup."

"I'm just loading the dishwasher." She leaned forward again and read the card. *Flee the evil desires of youth, and pursue righteousness, faith, love, and peace, along with those who call on the Lord out of a pure heart.* 2 Timothy 2:22.

The power of those words warmed her heart. With damp fingers, she reached up and flipped to the next card. *You have made known to me the paths of life; you will fill me with joy in your presence—*

"Allie, you don't have to wash dishes for me." Tyler's gentle rebuke startled her.

She glanced over her shoulder and saw him standing in the kitchen doorway. Plunging her hands in the soapy water, she began vigorously scrubbing a small frying pan. "I don't mind. Might as well make myself useful."

Tyler leaned against the doorjamb, his hands in his pockets. A small smile lifted the comers of his mouth.

"Thanks, I appreciate it. I'm not usually such a slob, but the last few days I've really been wiped out."

She blew out a deep breath. My, oh my, slob was not the word that came to mind when she looked at him. She silently chided herself and focused on the pan in her hands. What was the matter with her? She couldn't deny her attraction to Tyler, but starting something with him would be foolish. She'd made the mistake of following her feelings and trusting him before, and she didn't intend to get hurt like that again. Just because he memorized a few Bible verses, that didn't mean he had truly changed, did it?

"I think the soup is boiling." He pointed toward the stove. "Oh, right." She dropped the pan back in the dishwater and dried her hands on a towel.

Tyler suggested they sit at the kitchen table. He gathered up the newspapers and tossed them in a box by the back door. Allison placed his steamy bowl of soup on the table.

"Looks like there's plenty," he said. "Would you like some?"

"No, that's okay. I need to get back to the shop soon."

"Can you sit down for a few minutes?" He looked reluctant to eat without her, so she pulled out a chair and sat down.

He extended his hand across the table toward her. "Would you pray with me?"

Stunned, she slowly nodded and took his hand. His grasp was warm and strong.

"Father, thanks for answering my prayers for strength and healing." Tyler's voice took on a gentle tone. "And thanks for sending Allie here today to encourage me and bring me this meal. I'm grateful. You've poured out Your grace and love in my life, and I pray You'll give me a chance to do that for Allie. Please help us spread the word about Sweet Something, and we ask You to bless and increase her business."

Warmth and sweetness wrapped around her heart. She'd never expected Tyler to pray for her. Relief washed over her as she listened to the rest of his prayer. He certainly didn't sound upset with her. He probably didn't care that she'd cut their meeting short or that she'd gone out with Peter. Why had she even worried about that?

"Amen." Tyler squeezed her hand.

She squeezed back and opened her eyes.

He grinned. "This soup is making my mouth water."

She laughed softly and enjoyed watching his expression as he savored the first spoonful.

"This is delicious. Did you make it?"

"It's Tessa's recipe, but I put it together this time." She got up, intending to finish the dishes.

"Where are you going?" He reached out and stopped her.

She felt a tremor at his touch. "I thought I'd finish cleaning up while you eat."

She hoped scrubbing pots and pans would take her focus off Tyler. Because sitting across from him in this cozy little kitchen was making it very hard for her to keep her mind on the reason for her visit.

They carried on an easy conversation as she finished the dishes, wiped the counters, and put the extra soup in the refrigerator. His gaze followed her as she moved around the room. Was he comparing the way she looked now to their college days? She groaned inwardly at that thought. She might have more style and confidence now, but she

42

was also a little heavier.

After Tyler finished his soup, he stood up and stretched. The muscles of his broad chest expanded and filled out his wrinkly T-shirt. He certainly didn't carry any extra weight in the wrong places. She pulled her gaze away and searched for somewhere else to focus her attention. The photos on the refrigerator caught her eye, and she stepped closer.

"That's my niece, Emma. She's four. She always begs me to give her airplane rides or read her a story." Smiling, he pointed to the other photo. "And that's her little brother, Thomas. He's nine months and just learning how to pull himself up. He's big for his age, and he's got a killer grip. I bet he'll play football some day." He chuckled. "Sorry, don't get me started talking about them."

Allison smiled, touched by his description. "They're cute."

Tyler's eyes glowed. "Yeah, I can't get enough of that little Emma. She's a real heartbreaker. Hope I have one just like her some day."

Allison stared at the photo. Had she heard him correctly? When they were dating, he'd said he never wanted children. It had been a nagging difference between them that had never been resolved. What had changed his mind? She told herself it didn't matter and shifted her thoughts to her reason for coming.

She turned to him. "I'm sorry about cutting our meeting short the other night. I totally forgot Peter was coming over."

His smile melted away. "Have you known him long?"

"A little over a year."

Tyler nodded. "He owns that antique shop next to Sweet Something, right?"

"It's an interior design company, but he does carry a lot of antiques. His father started the business. He passed it on to Peter a few years ago."

"Old Princeton money." Tyler crossed his arms and leaned back against the counter, looking grim.

She smiled, hoping to lighten the moment. "Yes, and he likes everyone to know it."

Tyler's expression remained serious. "Is he a believer?"

Suddenly the room seemed too warm to Allie. "He attends Harvest Chapel with me."

Tyler studied her a moment, unspoken questions reflected in his eyes. "I haven't seen you at Harvest except for Christmas Eve a year ago."

"Oh . . . well, I usually go to second service." A little cloud of guilt settled over her as she spoke. That wasn't completely true. Since she'd opened her teashop, she only attended church one or two times a month.

"So, are you and Peter serious?"

Allison's stomach fluttered. "Well, we're dating . . . and we—"

Tyler held up his hand to stop her. "Sorry, that's none of my business."

Now she felt awful. "No, it's okay. I don't mind your asking. If you were dating someone, I'd probably ask you the same question." She chewed her lip a moment. "You're not dating anyone, are you?"

Tyler's gaze held steady. "No, I'm not."

Relief washed over her, then embarrassment. "Well . . . I'm sure there's someone very special out there for you."

Tyler nodded, a small smile lifting the corners of his mouth. "I'm praying for her."

Confusion swirled through her. What did he mean? Was

he talking about her? But she'd just told him she was dating Peter. She didn't want to give him the wrong idea about them, but if he knew how uncertain she felt about Peter, it might encourage him to pursue her again, and that would be—

"I'm sorry I haven't gotten back to you about the designs for your teashop. I still want to do that work for you."

"Oh, that would be great!" Relief washed over her. "I love that rose and teacup design."

His smile returned. "Good. I'll start working on it today."

"But you're sick. You need to rest."

"It's okay. I have my computer with my design programs here at home."

"If you're sure it wouldn't be too much trouble." She glanced at her watch and took the empty basket from the counter. "I better go. I don't want to leave Tessa short-handed for too long." She walked into the living room and picked up her jacket.

Tyler followed and helped her slip it on. "Thanks for coming."

She turned back toward him, suddenly wishing she didn't have to leave, or that she could do something else for him. "Would you like to borrow some DVDs? I could bring them by after work tonight."

"Thanks, I appreciate the offer, but I don't have a DVD player or a TV."

She glanced around the living room. His apartment was nicely furnished with a leather couch and chairs, full bookshelves, a computer desk in the corner, and original art on the walls. Money didn't seem to be a problem.

He grinned. "I know, that sounds weird, doesn't it?"

45

"I have a small TV at home you could borrow."

"Thanks, but I don't really want one."

She lifted her brows. "How come?"

"I used to complain my life was too busy, so one of my friends challenged me to get rid of it for six months. It was hard at first." He chuckled. "Guess I was addicted. But I like it now. And I have more time for important things like studying my Bible and reading."

"Oh." Allie didn't know what else to say.

"I've started running and playing racquetball again," he added. "And I've set aside a couple evenings a week to spend time with my mom and my brother Jeff and his family. My dad's remarried and lives down in Florida now, so I try to keep in touch with him by phone."

She stared at him. How could that be true? During the last few months of their relationship, Tyler's parents had finalized a messy divorce. Tyler blamed his father for his unfaithfulness, but he also scorned his mother for her vengeful response. Then he cut himself off from his family, and a few weeks later he'd left her, as well. She could understand the pain and disappointment he felt toward his parents, but why had he turned his back on her when she truly loved him and had tried to be there for him through the whole ordeal? Now he spoke to both his parents each week?

"Thanks for coming by. I'll call you when I have those designs ready."

"Okay." She walked out the door, feeling more confused than she'd been before their visit.

Chapter Five

Tyler rolled over, opened one eye, and squinted at his bedside clock. Surprise jolted through him, bringing him fully awake. How could it be ten fifteen? He'd already missed first service, and he'd have to hustle to make second.

Memories of his late-night design marathon resurfaced as he threw back the covers and climbed out of bed. That must be why he'd slept past his alarm—that and the fact he was still recovering from the worst case of the flu he'd had in years. But it didn't matter. At least all the designs for Allie's teashop were finished. He just needed to show them to her one more time, and then he'd send them off to the printer and sign company.

Rubbing his hand down his face, he headed for the bathroom. Maybe he could catch her at church and invite her out to lunch, or better yet, they could come back here and cook lunch together. He smiled. Sleeping in and going to second service might work out for the best after all.

His smile faded as he recalled the uncomfortable look on Allie's face when she'd tried to explain why he never saw her at church. They did attend different Sunday morning services, but why hadn't he seen her on Sunday evenings or at the singles' Bible study? What was going on with Allie spiritually?

During college she'd always been so certain about her faith. She was the one who'd patiently explained the importance of making a personal commitment to the Lord. It had taken him almost a year before he'd finally surrendered his life. Allie had been with him that night. But after his parents' divorce, he'd turned away from his faith and everyone associated with it. Thankfully, God hadn't given up on him. He sighed and looked in the bathroom mirror. Fine lines creased his forehead and surrounded his eyes, lingering evidence of the wild life he'd left behind.

But what about Allie?

The thought that she might have drifted away from her faith weighed him down like someone had just placed a thirty-pound pack on his shoulders. It couldn't be true. She'd never turn her back on God, would she?

Forty-five minutes later, Tyler walked into the second service at Harvest Chapel just as the first song began. He scanned the large sanctuary, searching for Allie, but he didn't see her.

Another wave of apprehension settled over him. Where was she? He purposefully shifted his thoughts to the words of the song. The music lifted his spirit, and he turned his concern for Allie into a prayer and released her back to the Lord's care, firmly reminding himself that's where she needed to stay.

His motives needed to remain pure. Build a bridge, ask forgiveness, help her business succeed. That's all. But as he remembered her visit to his apartment, her sweet, caring expression, and the way she'd prepared that hot soup for him, he couldn't keep from hoping there might be more.

The final notes of the song faded. Tyler glanced to the right. A couple moved into the row in front of him. Allie and Peter sat down in front of him, and his stomach clenched into a hard knot. Peter helped Allie slip off her coat; then he placed his arm around her shoulder.

* * * *

Allison shifted and tried to scoot a few more inches to the left, away from Peter. But he kept his arm around her and settled in a little closer. She sank a bit lower in the pew, wishing she could vanish.

They didn't usually sit this close to the front, but coming in late hadn't left too many choices. She hadn't realized Tyler was sitting behind them until greeting time when she'd stood and turned to face him. He'd said hello and reached to shake her hand. Her knees felt like noodles as she realized he must have seen every whisper and possessive movement Peter had made. She'd managed to mumble some sort of greeting before she sank back into her seat.

Allison silently chided herself and corralled her runaway thoughts. She was here to worship the Lord. Lifting her gaze, she focused on Pastor Tom's face.

"God wants more than just a piece of our heart. He wants all of it. Nothing should take His place. That's why Jesus says in Matthew 6:33, 'Seek first his kingdom and his righteousness, and all these things will be given to you.' " Pastor Tom's voice rang with passion and sent a shiver up her back.

"If you're struggling today, ask yourself this question: 'Am I honoring God and giving Him first place in my life?' If the answer is no, then I suggest you spend some time with Him, straighten out your priorities, and get your life back on track.

"I know some of you may say, 'Oh, Pastor, you don't know all the trouble I'm facing in my life.' You're right. I don't. But God does, and He is able to meet you right where you are and help you bring your life back in line with His Word and His purpose for you." Pastor Tom scanned the sanctuary.

Allison felt his gaze settle on her.

"You may have some painful choices and decisions to make. Trust God. He has a plan, and He is able to carry you through, if you will humble yourself and give Him first place."

His words pierced Allison's heart. She hadn't put God first or trusted Him to work out the problems with her business. She hadn't prayed more than five minutes about it. Instead, she'd worried and spent her time scheming, trying to use Tyler's friendship and free promotional help to get what she thought she needed.

Tears gathered in her eyes, and she bowed her head. *Forgive me, Father. I've been so wrapped up in my problems that I haven't even asked what You want me to do. I'm asking now. Please lead me and show me Your plans for Sweet Something. And what should I do about Peter? Am I dating him because Tessa says I should, or because he's rich and he knows everyone who's anyone in Princeton?*

Am I using him, too, hoping his money and position will somehow improve my business? Those thoughts turned her stomach. What had happened to her? How had she gotten so far off track?

Peter leaned closer. "Everything all right?"

Allison slowly lifted her head and nodded. He patted

her shoulder in a caring way, but it only made her feel worse. She closed her eyes and blew out a slow, deep breath. It was time she had an honest talk with Peter.

Two hours later, after an unbearably long lunch with Peter's parents and sister, Allison felt even more certain about her decision. She led the way up her front steps and stopped to retrieve her keys from her purse. Peter held out his hand and offered to unlock the door for her. But she clutched the key tightly. "We need to talk."

"I can come in for a few minutes, but I have to be back at the shop by three to meet a client."

"What I have to say won't take long." She bit her lip, then looked up at him. "I'm sorry, Peter. I don't want to lead you on. This just isn't working."

He frowned slightly. "What do you mean?"

"I can't date you anymore. It wouldn't be fair. We're worlds apart, and you deserve someone who appreciates you for all the fine things about you and your life . . . but I'm just not that person."

"I don't understand. How can you say we're worlds apart? We've both lived in Princeton all our lives. We both own businesses. We like theater, jazz, art museums, spending time with our families. What's the problem?"

"We do have a lot in common, but there's one important area of my life that I've been neglecting—and that's my faith."

His frown deepened. "But I've been attending your church for over six months, sitting through those sermons, learning the songs, and meeting all kinds of people I might never associate with." He wrinkled his nose slightly. "Doesn't that count? Isn't that enough to show you I'm interested in religion?"

Her heart twisted. "If I've given you the impression that an interest in religion is what's important to me, then I'm very sorry. My faith is based on a personal relationship with Jesus and a commitment to love Him and give Him first place in my life. Pastor Tom reminded me of that this morning in his message."

She waited expectantly, hoping it would click with Peter. But he looked more puzzled than ever. Regret weakened her resolve. She'd done more damage than she realized. No wonder he was confused.

She reached for his hand. "I owe you a big apology. I haven't been a very good friend or example of what it means to live the Christian life. I've been self-centered about everything. I'm sorry, Peter. Will you forgive me?"

He looked down at their clasped hands. "I care a great deal about you, Allison. I thought we had a chance to build a future together. Maybe if we just took a break—"

"No, I care about you, too. And that's why I'd like us to stay friends if possible, but no more dates."

His gray eyes softened. He lifted his finger and traced the side of her face. "Are you sure?"

She swallowed and nodded. "Yes, I'm sorry." She had no idea what the future held, but dating Peter wasn't the right choice for her.

He pulled her closer and pressed his lips against hers. The only thing she felt was a powerful wave of sadness, but she stayed in his arms for several seconds. At least she owed him that much.

* * * *

Tyler pulled into a parking place across the street and one house down from Allie's. Hopefully, he could catch her at home and show her these final designs. Reaching across to the passenger seat, he grabbed his computer case. As he turned and glanced toward Allie's house, he noticed a black BMW parked in her driveway and two people standing on the porch. His stomach clenched as he recognized Allie and Peter. Leaning to the left for a better view, he saw Peter trace his finger down the side of Allie's face. She looked intently at Peter, mouthing words Tyler didn't even want to imagine.

His heart hammered. Should he get out of the car and interrupt their little tryst on the porch? He reached for the car-door handle, but froze as Peter took Allie in his arms and kissed her. This was no friendly I'll-see-you-later kind of kiss, but one full of deep emotion.

A knife slit Tyler's heart. What a fool he'd been. Sure, he could say his motives were pure and all he wanted to do was help Allie's business grow, but underneath it all, he wanted her back.

Oh, Father, I haven't been honest about my feelings for Allie. But You've known what's been in my heart all along. I still love her. But she obviously doesn't feel the same way about me. Give me strength to deal with this, and help me let go of any claim I have on her. . . even if it's only been in my heart.

Chapter Six

Allison shifted her purse strap on her shoulder as she rounded the corner of Nassau Street. The bright April morning sun winked at her through the bare branches of an oak tree. She smiled at Tessa. "Looks like a beautiful day."

Her sister shaded her eyes and scanned the sidewalk ahead. "It's still a little cool for this time of year."

"It'll warm up later. I bet we'll be busy." Allison's voice lifted, optimism flowing through her. She could hardly believe the way her new commitment to put the Lord first had lightened her load—that and no longer feeling the pressure to try and make things work with Peter. What a relief. She hadn't realized how her anxious thoughts and gloomy outlook had weighed her down. Well, she was through with all of that now.

Tessa gasped. "Look, they put up the new sign!"

Allison lifted her gaze to the beautifully carved wooden sign hanging over the front door of the teashop. Sunlight reflected off the words SWEET SOMETHING, making the gold paint glow.

"Wow, it looks great!"

Tessa grabbed her arm. "You didn't tell me they were

putting in window boxes and planters. Oh, I love it! Tyler's a genius!"

Allison lowered her gaze and stared at the three large, wooden flower boxes hanging below the front windows, each filled with bright yellow daffodils, pink tulips, little blue grape hyacinths, and dark green trailing ivy. Four round cement planters holding the same colorful flowers lined the walk leading to the front door, giving their shop a fresh, inviting look.

Tessa gave Allison a hug. "Spring has arrived!"

Laughing, Allison squeezed her sister back. "I have to call Tyler. I can't believe he arranged for all of these flowers without even telling me."

"You didn't know?" Tessa stepped back, concern filling her eyes. "Those had to cost a fortune. Are you sure he isn't sending us a bill?"

"His assistant said there was no charge for the menus and business cards when she dropped them off last Friday, but she didn't say anything about the sign or planters."

Old fears sent a wave of uncertainty through Allison. What was going on with Tyler? She hadn't seen or heard from him in over a week—not since she and Peter sat in front of him at church. She'd called his office last week to thank him for the menus and business cards, but his assistant said he was in a meeting. He'd never called back.

"You better get in touch with him." Her sister bent and sniffed the flowers. "I suppose we might be able to keep these if they'd let us pay over several months."

Allison nodded. "I hope so. They're beautiful." As she climbed the steps and unlocked the teashop's front door, an idea formed in her mind. She turned to her sister. "Hold down the shop. I'll be back in a little while."

"Hey, where are you going?"

Allison smiled over her shoulder. "I'll explain later."

* * * *

Tyler stepped back from his desk and crossed his arms as he studied the enlarged newspaper ad he had created for the Grounds for Sculpture anniversary celebration. Hopefully, it would draw a large crowd and help provide the funding they needed to continue their unique work for another year.

His intercom buzzed. "Tyler, there's a delivery for you. I think you should come sign for it."

"Okay." The smile in his assistant Jolene's voice made him curious. He strode out of his office and into the reception area. Jolene stood in front of her desk with Mr. Sheldon's secretary Linda.

A deliveryman in neat khaki pants and green polo shirt stepped forward, holding a basket of plants and flowers. "Tyler Lawrence?"

He nodded and glanced at the basket brimming with shiny ivy, little daffodils, and tiny pink tulips. A miniature teacup and saucer sat on a mound of soft, green moss. His heartbeat kicked up a notch. It had to be from Allie.

"Please sign here." The deliveryman held out a clipboard.

Tyler quickly jotted his signature on the line and accepted the basket.

Jolene leaned toward Linda. "He must have a secret admirer."

Tyler cleared his throat. "Very funny. It's from a client." The women laughed softly and exchanged knowing looks.

He returned to his office and set the basket on the corner of his desk, then searched through the greenery and found a card tucked in next to the tulips. When he recognized Allie's feminine handwriting, his heart clenched. It had been a long time since he'd seen her write his name. He quickly tore it open and read the note.

Dear Tyler,

Thanks for giving Sweet Something a beautiful new image. I love the menus, business cards, and sign. The planters are gorgeous. What a fun surprise! Tessa and I would love to keep them, but we're not sure about the price. Please let me know. Thanks so much for using your time, talents, and resources to bless my business and me.

I'd like to make you dinner. Can you come over tonight at seven?

Allie

Tyler quickly scanned the message again. She wanted to make him dinner tonight? His hopes rose, but he quickly reined them in. She probably just wanted to thank him for the free work he'd done for Sweet Something. But as he grabbed the phone and dialed her number, he couldn't keep his hopes from rising.

* * * *

Tyler hustled up Allie's front steps. He hesitated as he crossed the porch, recalling how Peter had stood in that very spot and kissed Allie. His anger flared for a moment, but he shook it off. Tonight he was the invited guest. Not Peter. Hopefully, that meant there was still a chance—at least a chance to ask forgiveness and straighten out the past.

He knocked on Allie's door, then jammed his hands in his jacket pockets and blew out a deep breath. *Father, please help me keep my focus on You tonight. That's not going to be easy. You know how I feel about Allie. Help me want what's best for her even if things don't work out the way I hope.*

The door opened. Allie smiled and pushed back the screen door. "Hi, come on in."

"Thanks." She looked great in a red blouse and slim, black pants. Soft rose color flushed her cheeks, and her blue eyes sparkled. He realized he was staring, but she was beautiful. Not like a fashion model or TV star. Allie's beauty came from her heart and showed in her smile and caring ways.

As they walked into the living room, he noticed she had moved the two red wingback chairs closer to the fireplace and positioned a small round table between them. The table was set for dinner, complete with sparkling silverware and crystal water glasses. Three large white candles flickered on the mantel and a small fire crackled behind the hearth screen. Wow. She had gone to a lot of work to create a nice atmosphere.

He pulled in a deep breath. "Something smells great."

"Do you mean the candles or the beef stroganoff?"

He returned her smile. "Both."

Allie laughed softly. "Dinner's all ready. I just need to bring it in."

He laid his coat over the end of the couch, then followed her into the kitchen and offered to help. She handed him a basket of rolls. Then she took two dinner plates filled with beef stroganoff, mashed potatoes, and green beans from the oven, and they headed back into the living room.

As Tyler set the basket on the round table, he noticed a

Bible lying on the footstool next to one of the chairs. Stepping back, he took in the scene, and smiled. "This looks just like your painting." He motioned toward the chairs and table.

She set down their dinner plates, her eyes glowing. "I wondered if you'd notice."

Tyler fingered the white linen tablecloth. "This is really special, Allie. Thanks."

"You're welcome. It's the least I could do."

"And thanks for the basket you sent to the office."

She glanced at him as she sat down. "I wanted you to know how much I appreciate everything you've done. I hope that was okay."

He took a seat. "Well, I've never received flowers from a woman before."

Her cheeks flamed. "I told them to make it mostly plants and not to put on a bow. I hope it didn't embarrass you."

"No. It was really thoughtful. I put it on my desk, and every time I see it, I remember to pray for you and Sweet Something."

"Thanks." She stared at him and slowly shook her head. "I don't understand. What happened to you, Tyler? You're so . . . different."

His stomach tensed. This was the opportunity he had been praying for. "I'm glad you see a difference in me. I want to leave the past behind and build a new life with the Lord at the center."

"I'm happy for you. I really am. But sometimes I still feel tied to the past." She lifted her gaze to meet his. "I don't understand what happened to us."

The hurt in her eyes hit him hard. This was going to be

more difficult than he'd imagined. He sent off an urgent prayer.

Tell her the truth. Don't hold back.

New strength filled him, and the words became clear. "For a long time, I didn't understand it either. But over the last couple years, I've learned a lot, and I think I can explain it now." He reached for her hand. "But there's something more important than an explanation, and that's an apology. Whatever my reasons were for leaving, I know I hurt you, and I'm truly sorry for that. Will you forgive me?"

Tears glistened in her eyes. "Yes," she whispered.

He looked down at his plate, fighting the emotion tightening his throat. "I don't want our dinner to get cold. Maybe we should eat first, and I can explain more later."

She shook her head. "I've been waiting six years to hear this."

"Okay." He took a deep breath and blew it out slowly. "When I found out my dad was having an affair, I didn't know how to handle it. I couldn't get past the anger to the hurt underneath, so I kept it inside and pushed you and everyone else away.

"While my mom and dad were going through the divorce, I was fighting my own battle, telling myself I never wanted to be like my dad, but I was afraid that's exactly what would happen. All kinds of doubts ran through my mind. Could I be faithful to one woman for the rest of my life? Or would I crash and burn in the relationship department like my dad? Did I have what it takes to be a good husband and father? Or would I end up hurting the people I loved the most?

"Then seeing the way my mom tried to destroy my dad totally blew me away. They betrayed each other, and I never wanted to be in a relationship where that much pain was possible.

"So I could only see two choices for us—stay together, get married, and eventually end up divorced like my parents, or break up and avoid that possibility. I know that sounds crazy now, but that's what was going through my head."

She nodded slowly, questions still lingering in her eyes.

"I took a job in New York and made a whole series of bad choices that led me farther away from everyone I loved. Then about three years ago, I met a guy at work who really lives out his faith. We became friends, and I started attending a Bible study he was leading. He challenged me to recommit my life to the Lord, and go back and ask forgiveness of anyone that I'd hurt. That was tough, especially going to my friends in New York who aren't believers. Most of them didn't understand where I was coming from. But having a clear conscience was worth it to me."

"So that's why you came back and wanted to help me—so you could have a clear conscience?"

He swallowed, struggling to find the words. "Yes . . . and no. I owe you so much, Allie. If you hadn't told me about the Lord and loved me into His family, I don't know what would've happened to me. Even when I took off and was doing stupid things, I couldn't run away from God. I was part of His family, and He wouldn't let me go."

Her eyes glistened with unshed tears. "I'm glad. I prayed for you."

"Thanks, Allie." He took her hand again. "I have to be honest. There's another reason I came back." Looking into her eyes, he felt like he stood on a high cliff about to jump off into a choppy ocean. "I never forgot you, Allie. No matter where I went or what I was doing. You were always with me. I came back to ask your forgiveness, but I also wanted to see if there was a chance for us to be together again."

Her stunned expression made his heart take a dive.

"Oh, Tyler," she whispered.

Feeling like a fool, he dropped her hand. "Hey, it's okay. I should've known you'd be dating someone else by now, not sitting around waiting for me to get my life together."

Her blue eyes widened. "But I'm not dating anyone else."

"What about Peter?"

She shook her head. "We're just friends."

"Come on, Allie, I saw you kissing him right out there on your front porch."

Hurt clouded her eyes.

Immediately he regretted his tone. "I'm sorry. I wasn't spying on you. I stopped by to show you the final designs for the sign and promo pieces."

Her face was flaming now. "That was just a good-bye kiss."

"Well, if that's good-bye, I'd like to see hello."

"No, I mean I'd just told him good-bye for good."

Tyler stared at her, hoping he'd heard her correctly. "You're not dating him any more?"

"No, it wasn't working out. We had a lot in common, but he's not serious about growing in his faith, and that's important to me."

"So you and Peter aren't together?"

She shook her head and sent him a soft, sweet smile. "No, we're not. I knew it wouldn't be right for me to keep dating Peter, especially when I still had feelings for you."

He leaned back and blew out a deep breath. "Wow, I don't know what to say. I mean I've been praying and hoping you'd forgive me, but I didn't think there was much hope that we . . ."

She raised her finger and pressed it gently against his lips to quiet him. "I've been praying, too. And I always wished things would've worked out differently for us, maybe now we have a chance to see if they will."

His heart soared. He lifted her hand and kissed her fingers. "You won't be sorry, Allie. I've really changed. I'm a different man."

Chapter Seven

Tyler glanced out the passenger window at the spacious, green lawn of the Princeton Battlefield Park and turned to Allie. "Why are we stopping here?"

She turned off the car. "Close your eyes. I want to show you something."

"How can I see it if my eyes are closed?"

"Very funny. Come on, I want it to be a surprise." She sent him an impish smile that got his heart pumping.

"Okay." He scrunched his eyes closed, sorry to lose sight of her. "I wouldn't do this for anyone else, you know."

She laughed softly. "Good."

He heard her car door open, and then a few seconds later, his opened.

"Keep your eyes shut," she said, a smile in her voice. Grinning, he climbed out of the car. "I hope I won't regret this."

"You can trust me." She took his hand and led him across the soft lawn.

The early afternoon sun warmed his back, and the scent of freshly mowed grass filled the air. A light breeze carried the fragrance of some kind of flower he couldn't identify. "If I'd known we were going on a hike, I would've worn my boots and packed a snack."

Laughing, she squeezed his hand. "Don't worry. We're almost there." They walked another thirty seconds or so, and she pulled him to a stop. "Okay. You can open your eyes now." Tyler obeyed, then blinked at a sea of yellow daffodils stretching across the grass in all directions. The bright, golden flowers bobbed in the breeze like dancers on stage, their slim, silvery leaves flickering beside them. Tall evergreens at the edge of the park swayed in the breeze, providing a peaceful, deep green background. "Wow, this is amazing." He glanced over at Allie as she took in the scene.

Her expression grew pensive. "The Princeton Garden Club planted seven thousand bulbs in memory of those who died on September 11. The flowers come back every spring." She turned to him. "It's beautiful, isn't it?"

"Very special." He lifted her hand and kissed it. "Thanks for showing me."

"I knew you'd like it." Her smile warmed his heart.

He slipped his arm around her shoulder, and contentment washed over him. It had been an amazing three weeks. He and Allie had seen each other almost every day and checked in by phone on days when other commitments kept them apart. Even in that short time they'd made some wonderful memories together—walks across Princeton University campus, an organ concert at the University Chapel, quiet dinners at her apartment, a visit to the Princeton University Art Museum, and discovering their favorite flavors at a unique little ice cream shop in Palmer Square called the Bent Spoon.

These were some of the same types of things they'd enjoyed six years ago, but everything seemed different now that there was a genuine spiritual dimension to their relationship. They often prayed together to end the evening and enjoyed attending church together.

Tyler lifted his gaze to the field of daffodils again. Allie didn't know it yet, but he was working on some surprises of his own. In two weeks they'd celebrate her birthday, and he couldn't wait to see her reaction when he showed her the limited- edition prints he'd had made from one of her paintings. He felt certain it would launch her artistic career, especially since he'd already contacted art dealers in Princeton and New York who were interested in carrying Allie's prints.

"Thank you, Tyler," she said softly.

He looked into her eyes and read the message of love reflected there. Gratefulness washed over him. "Why are you thanking me? You're the one who brought me here."

She smiled at him sweetly. "Because sharing it with you is what makes it special."

He wrapped his arms around her and kissed her cheek. "You're the one who makes every day special."

Chapter Eight

Rain drummed on the front windows of Sweet Something.

Allison glanced at her watch, concern tightening her stomach. Six forty-seven. Where could Tyler be? He'd said he would meet her at the shop after work, then take her home to change before they went out to dinner to celebrate her birthday. She straightened the little packages of specialty teas and adjusted the row of teapots on the next shelf. She shouldn't worry. Tyler probably had a perfectly reasonable explanation for being late.

Then why hadn't he called?

Tessa stepped down into the gift shop. "Hey, I didn't know you were still here. I thought Tyler was picking you up at six."

"I'm sure he'll be here any minute. You can go. I'll lock up."

"Allie, it's almost seven. Are you sure he's coming? I don't want to leave you here without a ride."

"We have dinner reservations at The Blue Point Grill. He'll be here soon." But little vines of doubt wrapped around her heart, squeezing out her confidence and replacing it with old fears she couldn't quite shake. Memories of another rainy night six years earlier flew into her mind and sent a chill up her spine.

Tessa frowned and crossed her arms. "Did you call him? Maybe he got held up at work."

"I tried. No one's there."

"How about his cell phone or home?"

"I called those, too. He didn't answer." She wrapped her arms around herself as she stared out the rain-spattered windows. The glow from streetlights glistened on the wet pavement. Cars splashed through the puddles, making their way down Nassau Street. "The weather's awful. I hope nothing's happened to him."

"Maybe his car broke down again." Tessa glanced out the window and back at Allison. "Did you tell him how worried you were when that happened last time and he didn't call?"

She averted her eyes. "No, I didn't want him to think I was one of those clingy women who can't let her boyfriend out of her sight for more than ten minutes."

Tessa sighed. "You need to be honest with him. He should call if he's going to be late, especially on your birthday! We wanted to have a family party tonight, but we had to change our plans because he said he was going to take you out."

"I know, I know." Allison rubbed her forehead. "This is probably just a mix-up or something."

Tessa leveled her gaze at Allison. "I don't know what's going on. But remember this, people put their best foot forward when they're dating. And if this is Tyler's best, then . . ."

"Tessa, please. That's not helpful. I'm sure there's an explanation."

"Okay. I hope you're right." Tessa joined Allison by the front window. "Just don't give your heart away until you're sure Tyler respects you and cherishes you." She gently touched Allison's arm. "Think about it, okay?"

The clock by the door struck seven. Allison looked into her sister's eyes. "Okay. I hear what you're saying."

* * * *

Tyler pushed open the heavy glass door of his office building and dashed into the rain.

The limo driver of the Lincoln Town Car sprang into action and opened the rear passenger door for him.

As Tyler bent to step in, his cell phone slipped from his hand and splashed into a puddle at his feet. Irritation coursed through him. Fishing through the cold water, he retrieved the phone. He wiped it on his pants leg and gave it a good shake before he climbed in the car.

"Which airline are you flying with, Mr. Lawrence?"

"US Air." Tyler hooked his seat belt and flipped open his phone. Little drops of water fogged his screen and dripped from the buttons. He swiped his coat sleeve over the phone's screen and punched in speed dial for Allie at Sweet Something. Lifting it to his ear, he prayed it would work, but the silence buzzed back at him. A crazy mixture of fear and foreboding coursed through him. He had to explain things to Allie before he left town. He needed her prayers.

Sighing, he laid his head back and closed his eyes. Hopefully, he'd have time to call her from the airport.

Forty-five minutes later he hustled through the revolving door of the Newark International Airport and scanned the scene in Terminal A. Crowds of people, toting bulky suitcases, stood between him and the check-in counter. Tyler shot off an urgent prayer. He had less than thirty-five minutes to get through the line and onto that plane for Tampa. His stepmother's call left little doubt. His father's situation was serious. He had to come now.

He spotted a tall, blond agent, with a caring smile, helping passengers find the correct line. She listened to his story and took him directly to the ticket counter. In less than seven minutes he had paid for his ticket and had his boarding pass in hand. The same agent took him to the head of the security line. He thanked her and quickly made his way through the checkpoint.

Running down the concourse toward his gate, he spotted a pay phone. He hadn't used one in ages and soon realized he needed coins he didn't have. Dashing into a bookshop across the concourse, he tried to persuade the clerk to give him change for a five. But he refused to open the register unless Tyler made a purchase. He grabbed a bag of peanuts and tossed the five-dollar bill on the counter. The clerk passed back a handful of change.

Tyler glanced at his watch as he approached the phone. He had less than seventeen minutes before the plane took off. Frustration swelled in his chest. Allie must think he was a jerk for standing her up on her birthday. He wearily rubbed his eyes and pulled in a deep breath. He had to get a grip. She would understand. They'd been praying for his dad, asking the Lord to give Tyler an opportunity to speak to him about his faith. He just never expected their prayers to be answered like this.

He punched in her home number and waited for the call to go through. Gripping the receiver, he counted four rings, and then the answering machine clicked on.

Disappointment pulsed through him. He didn't want to talk to a machine. Emotion rose and clogged his throat, stealing his words for a few seconds. Finally he spoke. "Allie, it's me. My stepmom called from the hospital in Clearwater. My dad had a heart attack on the golf course this afternoon. She's pretty upset. She wants me to come right away. I'm at the airport now, catching a seven-ten flight. Please pray. I'm not ready to say good-bye to my dad." Tyler's voice choked off. He closed his eyes and swallowed. "I'm sorry about tonight." He stopped to listen as they made the final call for his flight. "I have to go. I love you."

He listened to the silence on the other end of the line, and his shoulders sagged.

Chapter Nine

A jumble of fear and frustration swirled through Allison as she stooped and picked up the Saturday morning paper outside Tyler's front door. It was almost ten thirty. Could he be sleeping in? Maybe he'd never come home. That thought sent a sickening wave through her. *Please, Lord, don't let it be something like that. She lifted her hand and knocked.*

Last night she'd finally given up waiting for him at the shop and left with Tessa. Her sister threw together a last-minute birthday party complete with a cake she pulled from the freezer and an off-key round of "Happy Birthday." Allison sang along for her niece and nephews' sake, but her heart wasn't in it. When she finally arrived home around nine, she checked her answering machine. There was only one message. It began with a long pause. She knew it had to be a telemarketer and quickly pushed the DELETE button. She was not in the mood to listen to a sales spiel.

She called Tyler's home and cell phone once more, leaving a second round of messages. Then she fell into bed and gave in to her tears. Lying there, staring at the ceiling, she tried to fight off the assault of accusing thoughts and painful memories. But the old fears of abandonment and betrayal rose to the surface, mocking her for believing Tyler had truly changed. She didn't fall asleep until well after midnight, and she spent the night wrestling through disturbing dreams. When morning arrived, she resolved to stop fretting and do something.

She knocked on Tyler's door again, but he didn't answer. Standing on tiptoes, she took down the spare key and unlocked the door. Tyler had shown her his hiding place above the doorframe last week when he'd been locked out.

She slowly pushed open the door and slipped inside, feeling more like a burglar than a concerned friend. She called Tyler's name and listened to her voice echo off the walls. A quick glance around the quiet living room and dining room revealed nothing unusual. She walked into the kitchen and spotted two coffee cups and a sticky cereal bowl on the counter. Looking more closely, she saw the cereal was hard and stuck to the bottom of the bowl. Definitely yesterday's breakfast.

A shiver raced up her back as she left the kitchen and headed down the hall. Peeking in the bedroom, she saw his empty bed. The blankets and comforter had been pulled up and straightened. A pair of white socks and gray sweatpants lay on the floor near the closet. She tiptoed across the soft, beige carpet and slowly pushed open the bathroom door. A towel, comb, and shaving gear cluttered the counter, but there was no sign of Tyler.

She walked back into the living room, running through all the possible explanations for Tyler's disappearance for the hundredth time. Should she call his mom or brother? The local hospitals or the police? Maybe she could find his dad's number in Florida, but she wasn't sure where he lived. Her gaze moved to Tyler's desk in the comer of the room. His open laptop sat in the center of the desk. A tropical beach screensaver slowly faded to a second photo with palm trees and aqua water. Allison walked over and touched a computer key. The screensaver immediately disappeared and a desktop photo popped up, filling the screen.

Her eyebrows lifted. She and Tyler stood arm-in-arm in the center of the sea of brilliant daffodils. She sank into the desk chair and stared at her own image smiling back at her from the laptop. She'd looked directly at the camera lens, but he looked at her. The affection in his eyes was unmistakable. Warmth flooded through her, relaxing her tense muscles. Tears misted her vision. How could she doubt his love?

She sniffed and glanced at Tyler's open Bible lying on the desk next to the computer. Leaning closer, she focused on a section Tyler had carefully underlined in 1 Corinthians 13. *Love is patient, love is kind . . . It is not easily angered, it keeps no record of wrongs . . . It always protects, always trusts, always hopes, always perseveres.*

Allison tilted her head slightly to read Tyler's handwritten note in the margin. Surprise rippled through her when she saw her name and the date of February fourth, over a year ago, written there. What did it mean? Had he been thinking of her?

Praying for her? It seemed strange since they hadn't even been in contact at that time.

She focused on the verses again, letting their message sink in. The unconditional love described there was built on choices and decisions, not just feelings.

Did she have that kind of love for Tyler? Her heart ached as she considered that question.

What should I do, Lord?

* * * *

Monday morning Allison hurried in the back door of Sweet Something and hung up her coat.

Tessa glanced up from arranging hot scones on a delicate blue china plate. "Good morning."

The question in her sister's eyes sent a ripple of uneasiness through Allison. She knew Tessa wanted to ask if she'd heard from Tyler, but she didn't want to talk about it. Her calls to the hospitals had turned up nothing. On Sunday, she'd left messages with his brother and his mother, but neither of them had called back yet. She'd made up her mind. If she didn't hear from him by the end of the day, she would contact the police.

Kayla breezed into the kitchen carrying a tray of dishes. When she saw Allison, embarrassment flashed in her eyes. "I'm sorry, Allison, Tyler just called a couple minutes ago. I told him you weren't in yet."

Allison's heart leaped. "Did he leave a message?"

Kayla set the tray by the sink. "He asked you to call, and he left a number."

"You're sure he didn't say anything else?" Tessa asked, her brows in a skeptical arch. "Like where he's been for the past three days?"

"Tessa, please." Allison turned to Kayla. "Where's the number?"

"Out front by the phone." Kayla led the way back through the teashop. When they reached the antique desk they used as a hostess podium, she pointed to the pad of paper next to the phone.

Allison's heart hammered. The number began with an area code she didn't recognize. She thanked Kayla as she grabbed the phone and quickly punched it in.

After two rings a mechanical voice answered. "I'm sorry, the number you have dialed is no longer in service. Please check the number and dial again."

She immediately tried a second time but got the same message. She blew out a frustrated breath and called Kayla over. "That number's not working. Are you sure he didn't say anything else?"

Kayla thought for a few seconds. "No, he sounded kind of stressed or something." She bit her lip and looked at Allison with an apologetic expression. "It was kind of noisy when he called. Maybe I got the number wrong. I'm sorry."

"It's all right." She sent Kayla back to work and stared out the front window. At least Tyler had finally tried to reach her. But what would he think when she didn't return his call? She closed her eyes, praying for guidance. The verses she'd read in Tyler's Bible ran through her mind again. *Love is patient, love is kind . . . It is not easily angered, it keeps no record of wrongs . . . It always protects, always trusts, always hopes, always perseveres.*

Conviction flooded her heart. She'd allowed doubt and fear to fill her thoughts. She had held onto Tyler's record of wrongs even though he'd asked forgiveness and shown her in so many ways that he was walking on a new path of faith.

If she truly loved him, she needed to forgive him once and for all and believe the best about him, even though she was unsure of the future.

She would need a supernatural infusion of faith and courage to love Tyler like that, with no strings and no guarantees. Assurance washed over her. If she was willing, God would help her. He'd promised to pour out His love in and through her so she would have a never-ending supply.

If love was her goal, she couldn't go wrong. This was her answer.

Later that afternoon, she noticed a stack of letters and a small package the mailman had left on the front desk. She sorted through the pile and pulled out the package. Reading the return address in the top corner, she smiled. It was from her friend, Haley Tannehill in Tulsa, Oklahoma.

Tearing off the tape, she recalled how she'd first met Haley and two other young, single friends, Monica and Angel, at the National Restaurateurs' Convention in Dallas almost two years ago. Thrown together that first night of the convention when they'd been stuck in the hotel elevator, they found they had a lot in common.

Besides attending seminars and walking the convention floor together, they'd shared several meals and confided in each other about their nonexistent love lives. After all, being in the restaurant business didn't leave much time for dating. At least, that's the excuse they gave each other.

Allison reached in the package and pulled out the apron with the words **KISS THE COOK** emblazoned across the bib. Smiling, she shook her head. How had Haley ended up with the apron? They'd all laughed when Angel tied it on to show it to them that last night in Dallas. She remembered how they had joked about passing the apron around among the group, but she didn't think they'd actually follow through. Looking closer, she noticed her friends had signed the apron.

Allison pulled out a folded letter from the package.

Dear Allison,

Here's a little gift for you! Hope it will remind you of the fun time we shared in Dallas. This apron has made the rounds among our little group, and I understand you are the only one who hasn't had the pleasure of wearing it.

Now don't you dare toss it out! It's had a wonderful effect on each of us.

Angel took it home and fell in love within just a few months of her return to Florida. Did you hear she got married last June? She sent it on to Monica who got back together with Gil, a great guy she'd known years ago. They were married in August! It arrived in my mailbox a few months ago, shortly after Scott Jantzen returned from his deployment overseas.

It worked, like a charm! Scott and I were married May first! So I'm passing it on to you. I don't believe it's magic, but I do think when you open your heart to all the possibilities and let the Lord lead you, some wonderful things can happen. I want you to tie it on and send me a picture! Don't disappoint me. Give love a chance . . . and see where it leads.

With love from the Cowpoke Cafe,

Haley

P.S. You are coming to the convention again, aren't you? Please, please say yes! And be sure to bring the apron!!

Allison lifted the apron once more. She smiled at the thought of her friends wearing it and falling in love. Would it help in her situation? She laughed at herself for even forming the question in her mind. She believed in Providence—the wisdom, care, and guidance of God—not lucky aprons. Still, what harm could it do to wear the apron and take a picture for Haley? It would remind her of her three special friends who cared about her and prayed for her. She slipped it over her head and tied it at the back. She would wear it for them . . . and see what happened.

Chapter Ten

Allison watched the older couple walk toward the front door of Sweet Something. The man slowed and took his wife's hand as she stepped down into the gift shop. She stopped to admire the collection of teapots, and he waited patiently by her side, listening to her comments with an affectionate look in his eyes.

It was well past six, but Allison didn't want to hurry her final customers out the door. They appeared to be at least seventy-five and obviously enjoying their time together.

As they walked by, Alison smiled and lifted her hand. "Come back and see us again," she called.

"Oh, we will. Thank you." The old gentleman held the door open for his wife. She passed through and took his arm. They exchanged contented smiles and headed down Nassau Street into the early evening twilight.

Allison's smile faded. Would she and Tyler share a love like that, one that lasted through the years? Closing her eyes, a prayer rose from her heart. *Please, Lord, take care of him wherever he is and bring him back to me.*

With a sigh, she turned off the outside lights, locked the front door, and flipped the sign to CLOSED. She glanced down at her KISS THE COOK apron and brushed off a few crumbs. Several people had commented on it, joking with her about the phrase. She had pasted on a smile and asked Tessa to take her picture for Haley.

A loud knock startled her out of her reverie. She turned and looked toward the front door. The reflection of the interior lights made it impossible to see through the glass. "I'm sorry, we're closed." She glanced uneasily over her shoulder at the empty teashop.

"Allie, it's me."

Recognition flashed through her. She hurried over and unlocked the door.

Tyler stood in the doorway, wearing jeans and a soft blue shirt and carrying a large black portfolio. He looked at her with a somber, almost haggard expression.

She greeted him with a tremulous smile. "Hi."

He walked in and shut the door.

She stepped forward and hugged him, but he remained stiff and unyielding in her arms.

Fear moved through her, tightening her stomach. She stepped back and looked up at him. "What's wrong?"

A storm brewed in his brown eyes. "What's going on, Allie?"

"What do you mean?"

"I've just been through one of the toughest times in my life. I needed you." His voice sounded hushed and strained. "Where have you been?"

Shock waves jolted through her. "What do you mean, where have I been? You're the one who disappeared without a word."

"I called you Friday night before I left."

"I waited here until after seven. The phone never rang. I went to Tessa and Matt's for my birthday, but the whole time I was worried about you."

A painful, confused look filled his face. "I'm sorry about your birthday. I called your house from the airport. I explained everything."

"What were you doing at the airport?"

"Didn't you listen to your answering machine?"

She lifted her hand in exasperation. "There was no message from you, only one that started with a long pause, and I knew—" Too late, realization flashed through her.

"That was me. I had a hard time getting started. I wanted to talk to you, not leave a message."

Allie sank onto the wooden bench. "I thought it was a sales call. I deleted it." She looked up and noticed the tired lines around his eyes. "Where did you go?"

"I had to fly to Florida. My dad had a heart attack."

She pulled in a sharp breath, regret tightening her throat. "Oh, Tyler. Is he all right?"

"He had to have surgery, but it looks like he's going to be okay." He raked his hand through his hair and sat down on the bench next to her. "My stepmom's sister, Barbara, came down yesterday. She can stay as long as they need her. So I decided it was time to come home." He looked at her with a renewed tenderness. "I missed you, Allie."

"I'm so sorry. I didn't know. I called your cell phone and your apartment. I left you a message each time. I was so worried about you."

"I dropped my phone in the rain on the way to the airport, and I spent almost all weekend at the hospital. I stopped by the office, but I haven't been home yet." He leaned back against the wall and closed his eyes. "Man, I can't believe this. We both tried to get hold of each other." He turned to her. "Did you think I'd taken off again?" His intense gaze focused on her, pain in his eyes.

She reached for his hand. "I was worried about you—and about us. I went over to your apartment on Saturday. When you didn't answer the door, I let myself in. I felt like a snoop, but I had to be sure you weren't lying on the floor with a broken leg or something like that."

Tyler nodded. "Of course I wasn't there."

"No." Allison smiled. "But I saw the photo of us on your laptop and the Bible open on your desk. I read the verses you underlined in 1 Corinthians 13. My name was written in the margin." She smiled. "Do you remember when you wrote that?" He glanced away, looking embarrassed. "I don't know. Awhile ago, I guess."

"You dated it more than a year ago in February. That was before I even opened Sweet Something."

His face reddened, and he rose from the bench. "It doesn't matter."

"It matters to me. We weren't even talking back then. Why'd you write that?"

"When I read those verses, I realized love isn't just a great feeling, it's a decision you make every day. When you love someone, you take action. You believe the best about them, and you put their needs ahead of your own."

She smiled, warmed by his words. "So you decided to love me back then?"

His gaze met hers. "I never stopped loving you, Allie. I just decided it was time to do something about it."

Her thoughts spun back to that time, the long hours she'd put into preparing to open Sweet Something, the money she and Tessa had scraped together to make it happen. A sudden thought struck, and she focused on Tyler. "Were you the one who sent me those anonymous checks?"

He glanced off toward the windows, frowning slightly.

She stood and faced him, certain she was right. "Tyler, please, tell me."

"I didn't want you to know."

She reached for his hand. "Why not? That was the sweetest, most generous thing anyone's ever done for me. How did you know I needed it?"

"My mom saw the article in the *Princeton Packet* about you opening your teashop. She cut it out and sent it to me. It arrived the same day I read those verses in 1 Corinthians. I started praying for you, asking the Lord what I should do. And it was one of those times when He put a very clear impression in my mind. He wanted me to send you the money." He gently tucked a strand of hair behind her ear. "I wanted to help you, Allie, but I didn't want you to think I was trying to buy my way back into your life."

"So you sent them anonymously." A sense of wonder filled her.

He nodded. "When I first moved back to Princeton, I used to drive by here and try and see you through the windows. I wanted to come in, but I wasn't sure how you'd feel about that. I sent my assistant from work in a couple times. She told me the shop was beautiful, but business looked slow."

Allison lifted her brows. "You sent a spy?"

He smiled. "Yes, but I had good motives." He wrapped his arms around her. "I love you, Allie. I couldn't stay away. I had to see you again."

She slipped her arms around his waist and rested her head against his chest. "I'm so glad you came back. Thanks for believing in me and helping me."

He held her for a few more seconds; then he looked

down into her face. "So, are you ready for your birthday present?"

She laughed softly. "You brought me a present?"

He nodded. Then he picked up the portfolio, took her hand, and led her up into the tearoom. "Let's sit in here." He chose a cozy corner table with a soft light shining overhead. "Why don't you have a seat right here?"

She smiled up at him. "What is it?"

"Close your eyes, and give me a minute."

She shut her eyes, heard him move a chair, and felt him turn the table just a little.

"Okay. You can open your eyes."

She did and gasped. Tyler had propped the open portfolio on a chair to display a large print of one of her paintings. The scene included a round, lace-covered tea table set with blue and white dishes and a large bouquet of pink, yellow, and white roses in a clear glass vase. "How did you . . . when did you?" She laughed. "I didn't even know you took it out of the closet."

The pleasure on his face erased all the earlier strain. "You like it? It's only the artist's proof. You need to okay it before they do the final run. And we have to make a decision about how many prints you want."

"I love it!" She rose from her chair and stepped into his arms. "It's the best birthday gift ever. Thank you." She kissed his cheek and focused on the print once more, her heart overflowing with gratefulness and love.

"You better sit down for the next one."

She turned to him in surprise. "You got me another present?" He nodded and looked at her with a serious yet tender look. "I planned to give this to you last Friday after your special birthday dinner." He reached in his pocket and pulled out a small, navy blue velvet box.

Her breath caught in her throat, and she was glad he'd made her sit down because her legs suddenly felt shaky.

"We've been through a lot over the last eight years. Looking back, I can see how everything that's happened has made me love and appreciate you more. Our faith is stronger now, and I believe with God's help we can make it through whatever the future holds." He knelt in front of her and took her hand. "I love you, Allie. Will you marry me?"

Joy flooded her heart, and happy tears filled her eyes. "Yes! Oh, yes!" She reached for him, and they stood and held each other close for several seconds.

Finally, he stepped back and opened the box, showing her the sparkling, heart-shaped diamond nestled in a vintage platinum setting.

She blinked to clear her vision. "Oh, it's beautiful!"

"Not as beautiful as you." With love shining in his eyes, he slipped the ring on her finger. Then he gave her a kiss, achingly sweet and full of promise.

When he leaned back, he sent her a gentle smile and glanced down at her apron. "Where did you get this?" Amusement twinkled in his eyes.

She told him the story, and they laughed about the effect it seemed to have on each of the women who'd worn it. "We have to add our names, too," she said, untying the apron strings at the back.

"I have just what we need." Tyler reached in the zippered pocket on the side of the portfolio and pulled out a black permanent marker.

Allison slipped off the apron and spread it on the table. He handed her the pen, and she signed her name.

He added his signature with a flourish. "There's one more thing we need to do."

"What's that?"

Chuckling, he drew a line through the word **COOK** and wrote **BRIDE**. "There, now it's ready for you to wear."

Laughing, they embraced again, but soon lost themselves in another delicious kiss.

"Are you hungry?" she asked when she'd caught her breath. He growled in her ear, making her laugh.

"I mean for dinner or dessert," she said.

He loosened his embrace so he could look toward the glass bakery cabinet at the back of the tearoom. "Do you have any lemon lush?"

She smiled and nodded. "I just made some this afternoon." "That sounds great. And tea for two."

"Sounds good to me." Then she kissed his cheek, tied on the apron, and headed for the kitchen.

SWEET SOMETHING'S LEMON LUSH

CRUST:

1 cup flour

1/2 cup butter, softened

1/2 cup walnuts, finely chopped

Mix flour, butter, and walnuts together, and press into the bottom of a 9 x 9-inch square pan. Bake 20 minutes at 350° until golden brown. Cool on a wire rack.

FIRST LAYER:

1 (8 ounce) package cream cheese (regular or light), softened

1 cup powdered sugar

Combine cream cheese and powdered sugar in a medium sized mixing bowl. Beat until smooth. Spread over cooled crust.

SECOND LAYER:

1 package instant lemon pudding mix

3 cups cold milk

Beat pudding mix and cold milk together with a wire whisk for two minutes and pour over first layer.

TOP LAYER:

1 cup frozen whipped topping, thawed

Spread topping over pudding mixture and form soft peaks. Chill for 30 minutes. Serves 12.

WHEREVER LOVE TAKES US

By Carrie Turansky

DEDICATION

To my husband, Scott, who shows me every day what
it means to truly love and serve one another.

*Thanks for thirty-five wonderful years and for
encouraging me to follow my dreams.*

"Where you go I will go, and where you stay I will stay.
Your people will be my people and your God my God."
RUTH 1:16 NIV

Chapter One

"**M**om! Watch out!"

Tessa Malone gasped and slammed on the brakes as an eighteen-wheeler slid in front of her van. The truck's rear red lights flashed, and she pumped the brake pedal, praying that would hold the van back from a collision.

"What a jerk!" Brianna, Tessa's sixteen-year-old daughter, scowled at the offending truck as it sprayed the van's windshield. "He ought to check his mirrors before he changes lanes."

The truck pulled ahead, widening the space between them. Tessa bit back a corrective comment. It would only increase the tension she and the children felt as they drove through the storm.

"This weather is crazy!" She strained to see past the foggy windshield and wiggled the useless temperature and defroster buttons. How many times had she told her husband, Matt, they needed to take the van in to have the defroster repaired? Why didn't he ever listen to her and follow through on things like that? Didn't he care about their safety? Did she have to do everything herself? She tried to put a lid on her resentment, but it bubbled like a pot on high.

Evan, her eleven-year-old son, tapped the back of her seat. "Mom, what time is Brie's orthodontist appointment?"

"Four thirty." Tessa glanced at the dashboard clock and blew out a frustrated huff. They were going to be at least fifteen minutes late.

Brie moaned. "Mom, you know Dr. Fisher hates it when we're not on time. He'll probably make me wait forever."

"Well, there's nothing I can do about that now."

"But I told Ryan I'd be home by five fifteen so he could call."

"Brie, please, I'm doing the best I can." Tessa pulled in a deep breath, trying to calm her frazzled nerves. The wipers beat out a furious rhythm, but they couldn't keep up with the torrent flooding the windshield.

This wasn't the best time to be out driving, but she had no other choice. They could only afford one car, so Matt expected her to pick up the kids from school, stop by the dry cleaner, return the overdue library books, and then take Brie to the orthodontist—all before going home to prepare and serve dinner in time for her and Matt to make it to the parent-teacher conference at Evan's school tonight.

She loved her family, truly she did, but working full-time and dealing with all their needs often left her feeling out of sorts and weary to the bone. But she couldn't imagine giving up her job. She loved Sweet Something, the cozy tea and gift shop she and her younger sister, Allison, had opened three years ago in Princeton, New Jersey. The shop was more than a moneymaking endeavor; it gave her a place to shine and use her baking and artistic talents.

"Mom?" Evan called from the backseat.

"What?"

"I think I've got a problem."

"What do you mean?"

"I forgot my science stuff at school."

"Well, you'll just have to call a friend and get the information from them."

"I can't. I need my papers tonight. The project's due tomorrow."

Tessa gripped the steering wheel. "Honestly, Evan, what do you expect me to do now? Turn around and drive all the way back?" Cornerstone Christian Academy was twenty minutes from their house on a good day with no extra traffic, and this was definitely not a good day!

"But, Mom, I really need those papers."

"I'll have to get them tonight when I go back to your school."

"Okay, but that means we'll have to stay up really late."

Tessa wearily massaged her forehead. Getting to bed before eleven wasn't happening tonight.

* * * *

Tessa heard the front door open. She glanced at the clock and then continued stirring the simmering spaghetti sauce.

"Dad!" Evan thundered through the living room. That set off Chaucer, their golden retriever. His excited barking added to the confusion.

"Hey, sport. How are you doing?"

From the sound of things, Tessa knew Matt was wrapping their son in a bear hug and squeezing him tight. For just a moment she wished that hug were for her. The sauce bubbled and splattered. She frowned and wiped the red spot off the stovetop.

"I'm okay," Evan said. "Except I'm probably getting a D in science."

"Why? You love science."

"Mom won't take me back to school to get my stuff, and my project's due tomorrow."

"I see. Well, maybe we can work something out. Come on, let's see what's cooking." Matt's briefcase thumped to the floor, and he walked into the kitchen. Lifting the lid of the largest pot, he sniffed and smiled at her. "Mmm, smells good."

It was just plain pasta again. Tessa wiped her hands on a dishtowel, ignoring his comment.

He replaced the lid and studied her for a moment, his gray eyes soft and welcoming.

"Did anyone get the mail?" Brie trotted into the kitchen, her dark brown ponytail swinging.

"I didn't have time." Tessa turned away from Matt's gaze and walked over to the refrigerator. Matt followed her and slipped his arms around her waist. She stiffened.

"What's wrong?" He rubbed his rough chin against her cheek. "Have you had a tough day?"

How about a tough three years? Tessa pressed her lips tighter. She would not say it in front of the children.

When she didn't soften or return his hug, he sighed, dropped his arms, and walked out of the kitchen.

Tessa shook off the wave of guilt. What did he expect? She had run around like a madwoman all afternoon taking care of everything their family needed, and now he was looking for a little romance in the kitchen. No thanks!

She had to get dinner on the table and then get them back out the door by six thirty. She jerked open the refrigerator and snatched the salad and Italian dressing from the top shelf.

"How long 'til dinner, Mom?" Evan picked up his basketball from the corner by the garage door.

"Five minutes. There's no time for basketball right now."

"Aw, Mom, please?"

"Evan, stop. Dad and I have to leave in a few minutes." Tessa deposited the salad on the table with a thump. "How about helping?"

He mumbled something under his breath and shuffled across the kitchen. "How many people?"

"Just four. Justin has a late class at the college."

Scowling, he rummaged around in the silverware drawer. Why did she always come out looking like the bad guy? Evan adored his dad and gladly followed any instruction he gave. But when she asked for a little help, he considered it torture.

Brie returned with a stack of mail and tossed it onto the counter. "Why don't I ever get any mail?"

Tessa lifted her brows. "You have to send a letter to get one back." She picked up the pile and sorted through the bills and junk mail.

A thick white envelope caught her attention. She lifted it from the pile and studied the return address. Why would a lawyer in Oregon be writing to Matt? A chill raced down her back. Was this another legal problem from Matt's business failure?

She'd warned him not to take on Patrick Stokes as a partner, but he hadn't listened. They'd ended up losing their home and been forced to move into this small condo. All the money from the sale of their house and their savings had been used to repay the disgruntled investors and prevent any lawsuits. What more did those people want?

Tessa's hand trembled as she recalled the terrible storm that had blown into their lives three years ago, nearly shipwrecking their marriage.

Matt walked back into the kitchen. He slowed when their gazes connected. "What's wrong?"

"I don't know. Why don't you tell me?" She tossed the envelope onto the counter.

A perplexed frown settled over his face. "What is it?"

"A very heavy letter from a lawyer in Oregon." She bit out each syllable and sent them flying at her husband like poison-tipped arrows.

Matt ripped open the envelope and pulled out the thick sheets of stationery. His gaze darted over the words as Evan and Brie gathered around.

"What is it, Dad?" Evan asked. "Are you in trouble?"

"No, I'm sure it's not . . ." Matt sank onto the stool. "I don't believe it."

Tessa gripped the counter, bracing herself for the terrible news.

Matt burst out laughing. "This is incredible! Unbelievable!"

"Dad! What does it say?" Brie leaned over his shoulder.

"It's the answer to our prayers. I knew the Lord would come through. I just didn't expect Him to work things out like this." He scanned the page, then looked up at Tessa. "Remember my uncle Don in Oregon?"

"The one who died last January?"

"Yes. I hadn't seen him since our family moved out here when I was a teenager."

"What about him?" Tessa wanted to grab Matt and shake

him. Why couldn't he hurry up and explain?

Matt smiled and waved the letter in the air. "It seems I'm in line to inherit my uncle's property on Lost Lake."

Tessa stared at him in stunned surprise.

"Where's that?" Brie asked.

"In the Cascade Mountains in Oregon."

"Wow, that sounds cool," Evan added. "A house on a lake!"

"Not just a house," Matt continued. "It's twelve acres of virgin forest with a large lodge and seven guest cabins."

Brie settled on the stool next to her dad. "So it's like a camping place or . . . a motel?"

"Well, I haven't been back there in years, but I'd say it's sort of a mountain resort. Uncle Don lived in the lodge and rented out the cabins to vacationers. It's a great place for fishing and hiking in the summer, and in the winter there's skiing nearby."

"But why would he leave it to you?" Tessa asked.

Matt glanced at the letter again. "He originally left it to his son, Charles, but he passed away before his dad, and the will was never changed. I'm the next closest relative."

Excitement tingled through Tessa. "That property must be worth a lot of money. How many acres did you say?"

"Twelve. And it's beautiful. Tall fir trees, cedar, vine maple . . ." Matt sprang from the stool. "Where's the atlas? Let's take a look at the map of Oregon."

"I'll get it." Evan ran from the kitchen.

Tessa clasped her hands. "This is wonderful! I'm sure it will be enough."

Matt turned to her, confusion in his eyes. "Enough?"

"Yes! We can buy a house and another car. And we can pay for Justin's college expenses and Brie's orthodontic bills." The thought of lifting the burden of debt off their shoulders made Tessa feel almost dizzy with joy.

Matt frowned. "What are you talking about?"

"Selling it, of course!"

Matt pulled back. "Tessa, you don't understand. This is like a miracle. I've been praying for a way to get out of this dead-end job and change careers."

"What?" Heat flooded her face, and her mind spun. "Matt, how could you possibly manage a resort in Oregon when we live here in New Jersey?"

"We'd have to move there." Matt rubbed his hands together, the excitement of a new challenge glowing on his face. "If we lived in the lodge and rented out the cabins, all the money we'd make would be free and clear." He stepped closer and took both of her hands in his. "Just think of it, this is our chance to start over, fresh."

She pulled her hands away. "Start over?" Panic nearly choked off her voice.

"Yes, it would be a great opportunity for all of us."

"How can you even think of moving? Our family is here. Our life is here." Tessa shook her head. "No! We've got to sell the property and use that money to get back on our feet financially."

Matt pulled in a deep breath and pressed his lips together. "Tessa, we can't throw away a great opportunity like this."

Fury built inside Tessa like a volcano about to erupt. "How could you even consider dragging us all the way across the country for another one of your harebrained business schemes?" Once she opened the vent on her anger, she couldn't stop the flow. "You've been praying! Well, I've been praying, too. We're barely scraping by on less than half the money we made before. And now you have the perfect opportunity to pay off all our debts and start rebuilding our lives, and you want to toss it all away on some silly childhood memory!"

"Tessa, come on." Matt's voice remained controlled, but she could see the color rising in his face and a muscle twitching in his jaw. "Look, I know this is a surprise, but I think—"

"Surprise! Oh no. What surprises me is that you care so little about what I want or what's best for this family!"

Anger and hurt flashed across Matt's face. He spun away and strode out of the kitchen. Her bitter words had hit their mark. Brie and Evan stared at her in frightened silence.

Guilt poured over her like hot wax dripping from a candle. It burned and coated her heart like a heavy weight. She tightened her fists and turned toward the stove.

Why should she feel guilty? Everything she said was true. This proved he didn't love her or the children. All he cared about was running after some foolish dream. Well, she wouldn't stand by and let it happen again. She had put up with more than enough from Matt Malone!

Chapter Two

Matt pushed open the door of the bagel shop. The jovial bell did little to lift his spirits. He scanned the small tables and soon spotted his friend Keith Stevenson.

"Morning, Matt." Keith pushed a steaming cup of black coffee and a cinnamon raisin bagel toward him.

Matt settled into the chair on the opposite side of the table, thankful his friend knew what he always ordered. "I got some great news."

"Really? You'd never know it by looking at you."

"Thanks."

Keith chuckled. "So what's going on? Were you up late with the kids?"

"No, Tessa and I had a fight last night." Matt took a quick sip of the hot brew. "Couldn't sleep much after that."

Keith's smile slipped away. "Sorry. I take it she's not responding to your plan to be more affectionate?"

Matt scoffed. "No, I'd say our relationship has gone from cool to below freezing."

"Well, hang in there. You've got a lot to overcome. We're not talking about a little sheet of ice that built up overnight. It's more like an iceberg. And it's taken three years to freeze that deep. It's going to take awhile to melt."

Matt cocked his head. "You're just full of encouragement today, aren't you?"

"I want to give it to you straight." Keith munched on his blueberry bagel and then looked back at his friend. "So what's the good news?"

He told Keith about the letter he had received from the lawyer in Oregon. "I'm now the proud owner of Lost Lake Lodge." Matt smiled in spite of his tired condition and the memory of his wife's hurtful response.

"That sounds great."

"Yeah. I want to move there. That's why Tessa's so upset. She doesn't even want to consider it."

Keith nodded. "Most women don't like moving. And with everything that's happened, I can see why she's not too enthusiastic about the idea."

"You should have heard her." Matt shook his head, recalling the stinging words Tessa had flung at him last night. There was no way he would repeat them to his friend. They were too humiliating.

"So what are you going to do?"

Matt blew out a deep breath. "I don't know. I want to win back Tessa's trust and love, but that seems just about impossible with the way things are going."

"Hey, come on. This is no time to give up. God is on your side. He wants your marriage healed, and He gave you this land for a reason. You just have to figure out how it all fits together."

Matt nodded and tore off a bite of his bagel. He and Keith had been praying together for the past few months and looking for practical ways for Matt to renew his relationship with Tessa. So far his efforts seemed useless. Tessa hadn't softened at all. But maybe this was all part of God's

101

answer—he just didn't see it yet.

"Let's do our Bible study, and then we'll spend some time praying this through."

"Sounds good to me." Matt reached into his briefcase and retrieved his Bible. He might not know what to do about the Oregon property or how to convince his wife to believe in him again, but he knew this much—the answers he needed were in his hand between the pages of this book.

* * * *

Tessa pulled the tray of apple walnut muffins from the large commercial oven. Their sweet, spicy fragrance filled the teashop kitchen. They were the fastest-selling muffins at Sweet Something, but she wasn't even tempted to taste one this afternoon. Last night's argument with Matt still tumbled around in her mind, setting her nerves on edge and stealing away her appetite.

Tessa's sister, Allison, walked into the kitchen wearing a white apron over her long black skirt and white ruffled blouse. She had pulled her golden brown hair into a low ponytail and tied it with a bright red ribbon. They hardly looked like sisters.

Tessa's olive skin and dark brown hair were like their father's. She wore her hair in a short, carefree style with fringy bangs that framed her face and fit her petite stature. Allison was taller and blue-eyed like their mother, and her movements always reminded Tessa of a graceful ballet dancer.

Allison reached for a tray of delicate teacups and saucers. "What time is that group of ladies from the historical society coming in?"

"I think they said three o'clock." Tessa absently laid the hot pads on the counter.

Allison studied her a moment. "What's going on?"

"Nothing. Why?" Tessa picked up a knife and began tilting each muffin so they would cool without getting soggy on the bottom.

"Come on, I know something is bothering you. You've been distracted and moody all morning." Allison stepped over and plucked a hot muffin from the tin. Peeling off the paper, she gave her sister a steady look.

Tessa released a slow, deep breath. She didn't want to tell her sister she might be moving, but how could she avoid it?

"I'm waiting." Allison took a bite of her muffin and leaned back against the counter.

"All right." Tessa huffed and set aside her knife. "Matt inherited some property in Oregon, and he has this crazy idea we should move there."

Allison's eyebrows lifted. "You mean live there permanently?"

"That's what he said. Can you believe it?" Tessa closed her eyes and shuddered. "I'm just sick about the whole thing. We had a terrible fight last night right in front of the kids. You should have heard him. He was going on and on about wanting to change careers and move out there like it was nothing more than a two-week vacation."

"Maybe he'll change his mind when he thinks about it a little more."

"I doubt it." Tessa thrust her hands into her apron pockets. "That man is so stubborn!"

"Funny, I never would've described Matt like that. He's always seemed like a pretty reasonable guy to me."

"Allison! How can you defend him? You know all the trouble his business failure caused us. Justin had to go to community college, the kids had to stop all their music lessons and sports, we lost the house and our savings. We almost lost everything!"

"Tessa. You had to move into a condo and get used to one car again. I wouldn't exactly call that losing everything."

"We lost a lot more than our house and savings. We lost our sense of security, and that's hard to restore."

"At least you have a family," Allison said softly.

Immediately, Tessa regretted her hasty words. Allison and her husband, Tyler, had recently learned they might not be able to have children. "I'm sorry, Allison. I know you're going through a lot, too."

Allison wrapped Tessa in a comforting hug. "It's okay." Then she stepped back and looked at Tessa with a sad smile. "I know this seems like a huge issue right now, but let's not let it rock our boat. Our anchor is firm. The Lord's in control."

But Tessa felt like a little boat tossed on a stormy sea. "Moving would be terrible. I don't even want to think about leaving Princeton."

"No one is moving today. This whole thing may just blow over. Let's trust the Lord and see what happens." Allison picked up her tray and headed into the dining room. "I'll go set those tables."

"Thanks." Tessa chewed her lip as she considered her sister's words. Sometimes Allison's spiritual strength amazed her. How could she hold on when her prayers went unanswered? Her faith seemed like a rock, strong and unshakable.

Tessa shook her head sadly. I used to be like that. But the last three years had left her feeling weak and beaten down.

But whose fault was that? She was the one who had slipped away from midweek Bible study, and she rarely took time to pray or read the Bible on her own. Sunday mornings were no better. She struggled to get herself out of bed in time for church and only made it to services two or three times a month. Matt and the kids went every Sunday, with or without her.

Allison returned to the kitchen. "Tessa?"

"Hmm?"

"Don't worry. This is all going to work out for the best."

Tessa forced a small smile for her sister's sake. But she couldn't shake the turbulent feelings swirling through her stomach.

* * * *

The phone rang in Matt's office. He looked up from his computer screen and rubbed his eyes, thankful for the break.

Though he had a degree in accounting and was a CPA, he hated working with numbers all day long. But as a supervisor for Ampler, Madden, and Politzer in the auditing and accounting department, he had no choice. They serviced small to midsized companies in the pension, not-for-profit, and manufacturing industries. The job held little interest or challenge for him, but it paid the bills and provided for his family. So he kept at it, day in and day out.

Matt picked up the phone on the second ring.

"Matt, it's Keith. You got a minute?"

"Sure. What's up?"

"I've been praying for you and Tessa all morning, and I think I've got an idea."

"Okay, shoot."

"I know you've been looking for extra things to do around the house to make it easier for Tessa, right?"

"Yeah, I spent all last Saturday cleaning out the garage." Matt turned his chair away from his desk. Outside his third-story office window, the first traces of golden-green leaves sprouted from the oak tree.

"What did she say?"

"Nothing. She's been bugging me to do it for weeks, but she didn't even notice."

"Wow, she didn't say anything?"

"No. She's too busy with the kids and the teashop to notice anything I do, unless I make a mistake, like forgetting to give her a phone message or taking the car when she needs it."

"I think it's time to bring out the big guns."

"What do you mean?" Matt spun back toward his desk and picked up a pencil.

"Plan something big, something she can't miss."

"Like?"

"Like a really romantic date. What does she like? French food, Broadway plays, classical concerts?"

Matt scratched his chin. "It's been awhile since we did anything like that. Money's been tight. We usually just rent a video or grab some pizza."

"See, that's what I mean. If you plan a really special date, that's bound to get her attention. She'll have to warm up a little."

"You think that'll work?"

"Yeah, women love romance. Trust me."

"Okay, I hope you're right, 'cause I'm in the doghouse and fresh out of ideas."

Chapter Three

Matt hopped out of the van and hustled to open Tessa's door.

She looked up at him with a perplexed expression, her dark eyes serious.

He smiled, glad she seemed to notice his gallant efforts. She looked great tonight. She wore a red and black flowered dress made of soft, gauzy material. It wasn't a new outfit, but he hadn't seen her dressed up like that in quite a while. Black beaded earrings dangled from her ears, and her lips were painted an inviting warm red. He had done a double take when she walked down the stairs at home, and he'd told her how great she looked. But she'd waved away his compliments as though she didn't believe him. Regret hit his heart. He hadn't complimented her often enough.

He let his gaze drift over her again, and it made him wish that she didn't hold herself so aloof every night. It had been too long since they had enjoyed each other as husband and wife.

Maybe tonight would help melt the ice. That was all he hoped for, just a little hint that she might be willing to rebuild the closeness they'd once shared. Of course he wanted more than that, but he was a patient man. He could wait.

Tessa glanced around as they stepped through the restaurant door and smiled. "I've always wondered what this place was like."

Matt held back a grin, thankful he had chosen the Lawrenceville Inn. A friend at work had recommended it, telling him the atmosphere was romantic and the food was excellent. He checked out the room and nodded. Tessa would like this. The owners had converted a historic home into a cozy restaurant complete with antique furniture, vintage lighting, glowing candles, and original paintings on the walls. The delicious smell of roasting meat and hot bread floated out from the kitchen, making his mouth water.

A smiling hostess seated them at a linen-covered table in the renovated parlor and handed them each a menu.

Tessa smiled as she glanced around the room. "This is very nice." Suddenly her smile faded. She lifted her gaze to his. "Matt, can we afford this?"

"Don't worry." He reached across the table and took her hand. Her cool fingers didn't move, and he wished with everything in him that he could change the choices he had made—they had cost them much more than their savings and home. They had stolen away the trust that had characterized their relationship for almost twenty-five years.

"It's okay. Tonight's special." He forced a small smile. "Let's relax and enjoy it."

Slight lines of worry still creased her forehead, and unspoken questions shadowed her large brown eyes. "All right," she said softly, then focused on the menu.

Tessa's silence shook Matt. Thankfully the waitress came and took their order. Tessa seemed to relax a bit when he asked her about the plans for her sister's upcoming art show at Sweet Something.

Matt looked up and smiled as the young waitress returned with their meals. He led in a brief prayer, then dove into his meal. Focusing on the delicious seared rib eye, he ate with only a few brief comments directed toward his quiet wife. About halfway through his meal, an associate from Matt's office walked up to their table.

"Hey, Matt, enjoying your dinner?" Jerry Fisher's eyes lingered too long on Tessa. "And who is this lovely lady?"

Irritation flooded Matt. Who did Jerry think he would be having dinner with? "This is my wife, Tessa. Tessa, this is Jerry Fisher from work."

She smiled and nodded, then lowered her gaze.

Jerry chuckled. "Well, aren't you a lucky man to have such a lovely wife."

Matt glanced across the table and read the discomfort on Tessa's face.

"Say, I heard about that land you inherited out in Oregon. What an opportunity. When are you moving?"

Matt clamped his mouth shut and glared at Jerry. This was the one subject he had promised himself they would not discuss tonight.

Jerry leaned closer, grinning like some stupid Cheshire cat. "So when do you think I should apply for your position?"

"I haven't made a decision yet," Matt said, barely hiding his irritation. Jerry had worked under Matt for only about six months. There was no way he had the skills necessary to step into Matt's job.

Tessa stared back at Matt with wide, pain-filled eyes, her face flushed.

"Come on, let me in on your plans," Jerry continued. "You are leaving, aren't you? I mean, that's what I heard from Ben Stackwell."

Tessa's chair scraped on the hardwood floor as she pushed back from the table. "Excuse me." She snatched her purse and hurried off toward the restroom.

Matt turned to Jerry. "I don't want to discuss this with you right now."

"Sorry, I didn't know it was a secret. Everyone's talking about it at work. You did tell your wife, right?"

"This isn't the time or place for this discussion. Now if you'll excuse me, I'd like to finish my dinner."

"You don't have to get huffy. I get the point." Jerry walked away, looking offended.

Good! That guy had a lot of nerve, bringing up that subject here at a restaurant in front of Tessa. What would she say now? Could he salvage the evening? He closed his eyes and shot off a quick prayer.

* * * *

Tessa took one last glance in the restroom mirror. No matter how much makeup she used, it didn't help. Her reflection seemed to shout: "You've been crying." Tessa sighed and pushed open the restroom door. She needed to get back to their table. There was no use pretending they didn't have a huge problem to work through.

As she reached the bottom of the stairs, a tall man stepped into her path.

"Tessa! This is a wonderful surprise." Bill Hancock's gaze traveled over her with a look of slow-warming delight. The recently divorced, forty-something owner of Hancock's Flowers made a habit of complimenting Tessa's creativity and baking every time he came into her shop for coffee. He seemed to notice each time she got her hair cut or wore a new outfit, things Matt never noticed or bothered to mention.

Heat filled her face. "Hello, Bill. It's nice to see you." Her glance darted across the room to the table where her husband sat.

"This is a nice place. I guess we read the same restaurant review." His blue eyes danced, and the dimple beside his mouth deepened.

"My husband picked it." Tessa nodded toward Matt.

Bill's smile faded as he looked toward their table.

"Why don't you come over and I'll introduce you?"

"That's all right. I don't want to interrupt. I'm in the middle of dinner myself."

"You wouldn't be interrupting."

"No, I'll see you at work tomorrow."

His meaningful look sent a shiver up her back, and then he turned and walked upstairs. Watching Bill go, she felt torn. This was crazy! What was she thinking? Bill was a friend, and her husband of almost twenty-five years sat across the room waiting for her.

She turned and wove her way through the tables to rejoin Matt and face the discussion she dreaded.

"Everything okay?" he asked.

She nodded and sat down.

"Who was that you were talking to?"

"Bill Hancock. He owns Hancock's Flowers across the street from Sweet Something."

Matt frowned toward the stairs.

Tessa could almost see the wheels turning in his mind. Did he suspect the way Bill flirted with her? Was he jealous? A little thrill ran through her at that thought.

Matt reached for her hand again. "I'm sorry Ryan interrupted our dinner. He's . . ." He shook his head. "I can't think of a nice thing to say about him."

"It doesn't matter." Tessa slid her napkin onto her lap. She'd lost her appetite, but focusing on her food was the only way to avoid the probing look in Matt's eyes.

"Yes, it does matter. I wanted tonight to be special. Just you and me with plenty of time to enjoy each other."

Tessa felt a little smile tugging at her lips. That was such a sweet thought. Not at all like the things Matt usually said.

"I didn't want to talk about the Oregon property tonight."

Tessa's smile faded. "Did you tell someone at work that you were leaving?"

"No, but I did ask Marlene how much vacation time I have coming. She wanted to know where I was going, so I told her I was flying out to Oregon to check out some property I inherited."

Tessa's stomach churned. "What about our plans to go to the Jersey shore with my family in August? We've been saving for that since last summer."

"I didn't say we couldn't go to the shore. I have three weeks coming since I only took one last year."

"And you want to spend that extra week in Oregon?"

"Yes." Matt looked at her like she was being very thickheaded. "How can we make a decision unless we take a look at the property?"

"We? You mean you expect me to go along?"

"Of course I want you to come. I think the whole family should see it. I'd like us to make this decision together."

Tessa laid her napkin on the table. "And how are we supposed to afford this trip?"

"We can work it out. I'll go on the Internet and find the

lowest fares. I'm sure I can get a good deal."

"When did you intend to go? We can't just pull the kids out of school whenever the whim strikes us."

"I thought spring break would be a good time. Come on, how long has it been since we've had a fun family vacation?"

"Exactly three years and five months." The wounded look on Matt's face sent a guilty stab through her heart.

"Tessa, I can't change what happened in the past. All we have is the future. Please don't be afraid to grab hold of this gift and enjoy it with me."

"Enjoy it? Matt, do you hear yourself? How could I enjoy uprooting our family and traipsing off into some forest fantasyland?"

Matt grimaced at her caustic words. "God gave us this property, and I think it's a great opportunity for our family to start over in a new place."

"Matt, I don't think this is a good idea." Tears filled her eyes as she laid her trembling hand over her heart. "It's just like last time. I have this feeling in here that it's all wrong."

Matt pressed his lips together, and a stern, stony look filled his face. "Tessa, I'm the leader in this family. I want you and the kids to come with me to Oregon to see this property."

Anger flashed through her, and she blinked away her tears. So that was what it came down to. He was pulling the old I-am-the-leader-so-you-better-submit trick. Tessa shuddered and glared at her husband. He didn't care what she thought. He had backed her into a corner. She had no choice at all.

Chapter Four

Tessa gripped the door handle of their rental car as they hit another pothole on the rutted pathway Matt had the nerve to call a road. She glanced at his white-knuckled grip on the steering wheel and his intense expression and could almost read his thoughts. I will conquer this road if it's the last thing I do!

They had landed in Portland two and a half hours ago, claimed their bags, picked up the rental car, and set off for the wilds of the Cascades and Uncle Don's mountain lodge on Lost Lake.

Tessa sighed and shifted her focus to the sparkling forest outside her car window. Snatches of clear azure sky peeked through the tall firs and cedars, still dripping from a recent shower. Lush patches of sword fern and leafy rhododendrons waved in the breeze as the car passed. Maybe a week in the mountains wouldn't be so bad. She might even enjoy it as long as Matt didn't pressure her too much about moving here.

"How much longer 'til we get there?" Evan called from the backseat.

Brie groaned. "Cut it out, Evan. You just asked that five minutes ago."

"Both of you pipe down," their older son, Justin, added in a disgusted tone. "We'll get there when we get there."

Tessa glanced back at her children sitting shoulder to shoulder in the rear seat. Justin's head almost touched the roof of the compact car. Cramming the kids in like sardines had already led to petty arguments and bruised feelings. Why hadn't Matt reserved a van or a larger car? Probably trying to save money. She closed her eyes and sighed again.

They hit another pothole. Tessa opened her eyes and gasped. Mount Hood rose before them like a mammoth, snow-covered pyramid, its jagged features reflected in the deep blue waters of Lost Lake.

"Check out that mountain!" Justin said.

"Let me see!" Evan squeaked, pulling on his brother's arm. Brie strained to get a better view. "Wow, it looks so close."

"The base is only a few miles away." Matt smiled and slowed the car. "It's really something, isn't it?"

Tessa nodded, stunned out of her disgruntled mood. She had spent all of her life on the East Coast and never imagined the rugged beauty of the Oregon Cascades. Matt slowed and turned into a private drive.

Tessa glanced to the right as Matt rolled to a stop in front of a run-down structure built of large rocks and rough timbers stained almost black with age. Tangled vines and tall bushes hid a good portion of the old building. Wild blackberry brambles obscured the front walkway. Holes gaped in several broken windows, and a gutter pipe swung in the wind, screeching a foreboding welcome.

Matt peered out the rain-spattered windshield. "Well, here we are."

Tessa stared at the startling scene. This was the lovely

mountain lodge Matt had described to her and the kids? Had he purposely lied, or was he unaware of the toll the years had taken on his uncle's property?

"This is it?" Brie asked, a shudder in her voice.

"Hey, it's not so bad," Justin added. "It sort of reminds me of a big log cabin or Swiss chalet. Look at those two stone chimneys. It must have a couple of nice big fireplaces."

"I think it looks cool!" Evan unhooked his seat belt. "Maybe it's even haunted!" He scrambled over his sister and out the door. Justin climbed out on his side and followed his younger brother toward the lodge.

"Wait for your father," Tessa called, but the boys only slowed a little.

Matt stepped out, then paused to stretch before he looked back at Tessa and Brie. "Let's see if we can find the key the lawyer said she'd leave for us."

Brie settled back in the seat. "I think I'll wait out here."

Tessa crossed her arms. *My sentiments exactly!*

Matt leaned back inside the car. "I'm sure it's safe; come on."

Tessa stared past her husband's shoulder and tried to swallow the panic rising in her throat. How could he look so happy? She knew the old place was probably full of spiders and snakes—maybe something worse.

Matt offered Tessa his hand.

She couldn't sit in the car all day, looking like a scaredy-cat, so she braced herself and climbed out. Brie followed, mumbling something about bats and the ghost of Bigfoot.

Justin whistled. "Hey, Dad, check out those wheels."

Tessa followed Justin's gaze and spotted a sleek black BMW partially hidden by the bushes at the side of the

117

house.

The front door squeaked open, and a blond woman in a long navy raincoat stepped out on the porch. "Hello there, you must be the Malones."

The woman had a flawless complexion and stunning blue eyes. She was at least ten years younger than Tessa and gorgeous by anyone's standards. Little vines of envy wove around Tessa's heart, making her feel like a dowdy pigmy.

Matt leaped up on the porch and reached to shake the woman's hand. "Yes, I'm Matt Malone, and this is my wife, Tessa, and our children, Justin, Brie, and Evan." The woman sent him a slow, seductive smile.

Tessa's stomach clenched.

"I'm Mallory Willard, your late uncle's lawyer." She released Matt's hand and flipped her long hair over her shoulder. "I got your message at the office, and I thought I'd drive out and meet you. How was your trip?"

"Great. Smooth flight. No problems."

"Wonderful." Mallory nodded and smiled.

Matt glanced around the porch and ran his hand over the sagging railing, looking as though he was assessing the repair work that needed to be done.

"Why don't we go inside, and I'll give you a tour?" Mallory's voice sounded as smooth as warm honey.

Tessa shivered and pulled her navy wool jacket closer. She followed Matt and Mallory inside, and the kids trooped in behind. As she stepped into the living room, a damp, musty smell assaulted her nose, making her long to throw open a window and let in some fresh air.

"Your uncle was quite a recluse. He said he'd lived here by himself for the last thirty-two years."

Matt nodded. "He always said he didn't mind living on his own, but it sounds like a pretty lonely lifestyle to me."

Tessa's gaze traveled around the large rectangular room, taking in every depressing detail. Cobwebs clung to the light fixtures and stair railings. An overstuffed, red plaid couch and two mismatched chairs with sagging stuffing sat facing the hearth. Cluttered bookshelves and a sturdy roll top desk occupied one corner near the large stone fireplace. A coffee mug and stacks of papers sat on the open desk as though someone had walked away and intended to return.

The thought that no one had lived here since Matt's uncle's death sent goose bumps racing up her arms. The sooner they finished this tour and were on their way, the better. But how would she convince her husband to abandon his plan of spending the entire week here?

Matt laid his hands on the back of the old sagging couch and stared into the cold fireplace, a wistful smile on his face. "I remember sitting right here and listening to my uncle tell stories about being on the Mount Hood Ski Patrol. Then there were all his hunting and fishing stories." He chuckled and shook his head.

Mallory smiled. "I'm glad you have such pleasant memories of your uncle. He loved this property. But his health declined the last few years. I suppose that's why he let the place go a little."

Shock waves rippled through Tessa. "A little?" Everyone turned toward her, and her face flamed, but she continued. "This place is falling apart. Just look at it." She waved her hand in a broad arc. "It would take thousands of dollars to make it livable." She glared at Mallory. "What do you expect us to do with it?"

"Well, that's entirely up to you and your husband." Mallory's gaze shifted to Matt. "It does need some cleanup and repairs, but I'm sure you can see the value and potential."

"Of course." Matt nodded and sent Tessa a sideways glance that seemed to question her sanity.

Tessa fought to keep her mouth closed. Mallory Willard didn't care how much effort and expense it would take to repair this lodge. She would have to be paid whether they sold the property or not.

"Shall we continue our tour?" Mallory led them through the dining room past a sturdy pine table and chairs and into the large kitchen. "I know your uncle was a widower. I suppose he didn't like to spend too much time in the kitchen."

Tessa stared at the grease-stained, rooster-patterned wallpaper and the chipped yellow cabinets. A small sink hung from the wall at an odd angle, surrounded by red Formica counters. An ancient refrigerator and a cast-iron woodstove filled the rest of the wall space. How could anyone cook anything edible under these conditions? She sent her husband a heated glance.

"All the bedrooms are on the second floor," Mallory continued, leaving the forlorn kitchen and leading them back into the living room and up the wide wooden stairs.

Evan ran ahead. Brie and Justin hurried after him.

"Hey, I want this room," Brie called. "It has a great view of the lake."

"This one has bunk beds!" Evan leaned out the second bedroom door and looked at her with pleading eyes. "Can I sleep on top, Mom? Please? I promise I won't fall off."

"We'll talk about that later." Matt gave Evan a look that said no argument allowed.

Justin disappeared into the next room, and Tessa heard

him opening drawers and rummaging around.

"Here's the fourth bedroom." Mallory pushed open the door and stood back for Matt and Tessa to enter.

Tessa held her breath and peeked inside. To her surprise, it looked a little better than the other rooms they'd passed through. Three large windows on the south wall flooded the room with warm light. A cozy blue quilt covered a metal-framed double bed, and an old pine dresser sat in the corner. An oval braided rug covered a large portion of the hardwood floor, giving the room a welcoming appeal.

"This is nice." Matt turned to Tessa.

She knew he wanted her to say something positive. It was the best room in the house. That wasn't saying much, but at least—

A little brown mouse dashed across the floor near Tessa's feet. She screamed and jumped back, bumping into Matt. He reached out to steady her.

Mallory gasped.

Matt lunged and stomped his foot, missing the mouse by several inches. The frightened little critter spun in a circle, skittered across the floor, and disappeared into a large crack by the baseboard in the corner.

Justin dashed into the room. "What's going on?"

"Mom, are you okay?" Brie hurried in behind Justin.

Evan slid in past his siblings. "What did I miss?"

"It's all right." Matt put his arm around Tessa's shoulders. "Your mom saw a mouse."

"Mom screamed 'cause of a mouse?" Evan cocked his head, looking puzzled. "Why'd you do that? You used to like my pet mice."

Tessa sighed. "I know. He surprised me, that's all."

"I'm sure you can get some traps from the hardware store in town," Mallory said.

"Traps?" Evan squeaked, looking horrified. "We don't want to kill them!"

Tessa knew their young son's sensitive spirit couldn't tolerate cruelty to any living creature, even stray field mice. She shot a quick look at Matt, sending a silent message.

Matt's gaze met Tessa's for a split second, then turned to Mallory. "We'll see if we can find traps that catch them alive, and then we can release them in the woods."

"Whew!" Evan pushed his straight brown hair off his forehead. "For a minute there, I thought our family was going to be guilty of mice murder."

Brie leaned closer to her father. "Good move, Dad." Adoration shone in her eyes. Then she placed her hands on her brother's shoulders. "Come on, Evan. I want to show you the view from my room."

Mallory turned to Matt. "I guess your children are real animal lovers."

"Yes, they are."

"They seem like great kids," Mallory added.

"Thanks. We think we're pretty blessed." Matt smiled and squeezed Tessa's shoulder. His eyes glowed, sending a private message that sent tingles through her.

For some silly reason her throat tightened, and she felt tears prick her eyes. What was the matter with her? Of course their kids were great. She knew that. And her husband was pretty special, too. Tessa returned a tremulous smile. Sure, Matt was a crazy dreamer, but sometimes she wished she believed in his dreams. Maybe then they could recapture some of what they'd lost.

Chapter Five

With a sleepy yawn, Tessa rolled over and pushed the blankets away from her face. Soft morning light filtered through unfamiliar windows. So it wasn't a dream. She really was in Oregon. A smile played at her lips as she remembered the special time she and Matt had shared the night before. If only he would give up this crazy idea of them moving to Oregon. Maybe things could settle down and they could focus on making their relationship a priority.

She squinted, searching the room for her husband. Why was it so hazy? She sniffed and sat up. Could that be smoke?

"Matt?" She climbed out of bed, her senses coming fully awake when her bare feet hit the cold floor. "Matt!"

No answer. Her heart began to pound. Could the lodge be on fire? Her mind fought to grab hold of reality. She snatched her robe from the end of the bed and slipped it on. When she pushed open her bedroom door, a thin bluish haze hung in the air, heightening her fears.

"Justin, Brianna!" Tessa hurried down the hall. "Wake up!"

Her older son appeared at his bedroom door dressed in sweats and an old T-shirt.

123

"Put on your shoes and get your brother," Tessa ordered.

Brie opened her door. "What's going on?"

"I smell smoke. Put on a sweatshirt and get your sneakers." Tessa dashed back to her bedroom and slid on her shoes. She returned to the hall in time to see Justin ushering Evan toward the stairway. Brie trotted down the steps just ahead of her brothers.

"Where's the fire?" Evan asked, excitement lighting up his young face.

"We don't know. Just keep moving," Justin ordered, hustling his brother ahead.

Brie slowed halfway down the stairs and looked back. "Where's Daddy?" Her pale face and wide-eyed look made Tessa's heart lurch.

"I don't know, honey. Just keep going. We'll find him."

The hazy curtain thickened as they reached the living room. Tessa shot a glance toward the fireplace, hoping she would find it was the source of the smoke, but it sat cold and empty.

Justin shoved Evan toward her. "You take Evan and Brie out front. I'm going to find Dad." The determined look in his eyes sent a tremor through Tessa.

"No, I'll find him." Tessa steered Evan back toward his brother. "I want all three of you to go outside."

"Shouldn't we call 9-1-1?" Brie coughed and squinted against the smoke.

Tessa grabbed her cell phone from the table. "Here, Justin, take my phone. Give me a couple minutes, and then make the call. Now go!"

Justin grabbed the phone and urged his younger siblings out the door. Tessa bent lower and headed toward the kitchen door where the smoke seemed thicker.

Oh, Lord, please help me find Matt. And I know I said I don't want to live here, but I didn't mean I wanted the place to burn down!

Tessa pushed open the swinging door to the kitchen, and her prayer came to an abrupt halt. Matt stood in the center of the smoky room waving an old dishtowel, red-faced and coughing. Smoke poured from the cracks in the stovepipe of the woodstove.

"What are you doing?" Tessa stammered.

"I'm trying to cook breakfast. But this crazy stove is impossible." Matt reached for the cast-iron frying pan full of half-congealed eggs. "I don't understand it. The fire is roaring, but there's not much heat coming out on top."

"Did you open the vents?" Tessa blinked against the stinging smoke.

"What vents?"

"There must be dampers or something. You probably have to open them like a flue on a fireplace chimney." Tessa coughed as she walked closer to the belching black stove. "Here, let's try this thing." She turned a handle near the firebox and stood back. Immediately the smoke stopped flowing out of the pipe cracks.

"Oh. I never saw that." Matt strode to the back door and shoved it open.

"I'll open a window." Tessa struggled to raise the window over the sink. Looking outside, she saw her three children huddled together by their rental car, anxiously watching the lodge.

"It's okay," Tessa called through the dirty screen. "You can come back inside. It's just your father—cooking breakfast." They groaned in unison and shuffled toward the lodge.

"What are they doing out there?"

125

"I smelled smoke upstairs and thought the lodge was on fire."

Matt turned toward her. "Sorry. I didn't realize the smoke had drifted all the way upstairs. That must've been an awful way to wake up."

A smile tugged at her lips as she watched her husband stir the pan of half-cooked eggs, his apron stained with soot. "It looks like your breakfast plans backfired."

Matt tossed aside the potholder with a mischievous grin. "Backfired. Ha! That's very funny."

Tessa covered her mouth to hide her snicker.

"Hey, I think I deserve a little appreciation since I've been slaving over a not-so-hot stove to make you this gourmet breakfast." His eyes glowed with warmth and humor as he walked toward her. "Come here."

She met him in the middle.

Matt wrapped his strong arms around her. He smelled deliciously like wood smoke and spicy aftershave. His embrace tightened. "I'm sorry, Tessa. I didn't mean to scare you or the kids." He sighed into her hair. "I never meant to hurt you. Never."

Was it the smoke or his tender words that brought tears to her eyes? She blinked them away and pulled in a shuddering breath. She could easily forgive him for this smoky breakfast, but how could she let go of the painful memories and trust him again after all his failures had cost them?

* * * *

Matt pushed aside his empty plate and settled back to enjoy his coffee. Tessa had come to his rescue in the kitchen, and working together, they had managed to prepare an edible breakfast. The kids gobbled up their food like hungry lumberjacks. Matt smiled. He had always heard that mountain air made people feel hungrier. The old saying seemed to hold true for his crew.

"This jam is good." Evan licked his lips and popped the last bite of toast into his mouth.

Tessa smiled and reached over with her napkin to wipe a purple smear off Evan's cheek. "So you like boysenberry?"

Evan grinned. "Uh-huh."

"Want me to finish up these eggs?" Justin asked.

"Sure, go ahead." Tessa looked at her daughter. "Unless you want some more, Brie."

"No, thanks. I'm full." Brie drank the last of her orange juice. "That was pretty good. Thanks."

Matt nodded. This beat their normal cereal-and-milk routine by a mile. That was all they had time for most mornings, before they all rushed off to their separate lives.

Evan scooted back from the table. "When can we go down to the lake?"

Tessa frowned. "I don't want you going down there by yourself, Evan."

"I'll go with him." Brie wiped her hands on a napkin.

"I'm ready to do some exploring," Justin added.

Matt held back a surprised grin. Back in Princeton, Justin preferred spending time with his friends rather than his siblings. Here was another good reason for them to move to a quiet, rural setting where they could all spend more time together.

"Okay, but I want you to stick together, and don't go in the water." Tessa bit her lip, an anxious frown creasing her forehead.

Justin rolled his eyes. "Mom, that water is probably

freezing. There's no way we'd go in."

"Not unless I push you." Brie grinned.

"Oh yeah? Just try it!" Justin gave her a playful shove as they headed toward the door.

"Wait, don't forget your jackets," Tessa called.

"I won't be cold," Evan insisted, plucking at his green sweatshirt. "I've got two layers."

"I know, but I don't want you—"

Matt laid his hand gently on her arm. "Let them go, honey. They'll be fine." Tessa's worried frown squelched everyone's joy. He wished he could help her relax and trust someone—anyone. Why was she always on guard like that? Of course he was thankful she was a caring, responsible mother, but Tessa's caring often slipped over the line into overprotective anxiety.

He sat back, watching the kids clatter across the porch and disappear down the shady path leading to the lake.

"I hope they stay together," she said. "I can't imagine Justin slowing down when Evan wants to catch a frog or a turtle."

"They'll be okay. I'm glad they're occupied for a while. That'll give us time to talk."

Tessa shot him a wary glance. "About what?"

Matt clasped his hands and rested his elbows on the table. "We've known about this property for six weeks. It's time to make some decisions."

"What do you want me to say?"

"I want to hear what you're thinking." He smiled, hoping her responsiveness last night was also an indication she was softening toward him—and his desire to move.

Tessa looked at him with a guarded expression. "I know you love this place, but I think we should do some cleanup, find a good Realtor, and list it. I'm sure some developer or nature lover will snap it up."

As her words sunk in, his throat ached with defeat. "You still want to sell?"

"Of course I want to sell," she said with an irritated huff. "We'd have to totally renovate if we were going to live here. And that would take too much time and money." She sent him a pointed look. "Money we don't have."

His anger flared, and he shot off a prayer for patience. "I know we'd have to put a lot of sweat equity into this place to make it nice enough for our family, but look at the property. There's nothing like this in New Jersey. And we'd own it free and clear, unlike that dinky condo we're renting now. Everything we put into this place would be ours, and with a little help from a few people, we could get the work done and open by midsummer."

"Open? What do you mean?"

Matt swallowed. Maybe he had made a mistake by waiting until they arrived here to spring this part of the idea on her, but she'd refused to discuss it at home. "I want to rent out the cabins as soon as possible and then build a meeting room and dining hall so we can accommodate groups by next summer. I've researched it and done a complete business proposal. I even have a few people in mind who might be willing to get involved as investors."

Tessa's eyes widened. "You can't be serious. How could you even consider asking other people to get involved in this—this disaster? Look at this place!" She waved her hand toward the broken front window, sagging curtains, and peeling wallpaper. "We're talking about thousands of dollars for renovations, with no idea how or when we would be able to pay them back. No, Matt!" Tessa sprang from her chair and retreated to the living room.

Matt followed her, but he paused to pick up a folder from the coffee table. "Sit down with me and take a look at these plans."

Tessa silently stared into the cold fireplace.

"Tessa, please. Listen to me. Share my dream." His voice grew thick with emotion. "I know I've made some mistakes before, but I believe the Lord gave us this property for a reason."

She spun and faced him. "Yes, He did. He gave it to us so we could pay off the van, get a decent home again, and be able to send our kids to college."

Matt growled and flopped down on the couch. "This isn't about Lost Lake Lodge, is it? It's about what happened before."

"No!" But her indignant scowl and quick answer confirmed he was right.

His pulse pounded in his temple. "When are you going to forgive me and let it go?"

"How can I, when you're ready to turn right around and do the same thing all over again?"

"How can you say that? You haven't even looked at the plans."

"Because I know you, Matt. You're a dreamer with your head in the clouds, while your family is down here scraping by, just trying to survive."

Angry words boiled up inside him, threatening to overflow at her painful exaggerations. Their lifestyle was a far cry from scraping by. They had both worked hard to overcome their financial problems, and they were making good progress.

"You don't trust me. That's the real problem. You don't

believe I have enough common sense and business know-how to make this work." He clutched the folder holding the detailed plans he had created to provide protection for them and any investors who joined them in developing the property. But she wouldn't even look at them. Her heart was as hard as granite.

"You're wrong about me, Tessa. I may be a dreamer, but I love you and the kids, and I want what's best for our family. I've slaved away for three years at a job I hate to provide for us and dig us out of this hole."

His hand shook as he pointed at her. "The real issue is you're afraid to take a risk. Even when God dumps a diamond in your lap, you run away screaming, 'The sky is falling!' "

Tessa gasped. "Oh, you're so—"

"No! Don't say anything else you'll regret." He got up and walked out the front door, slamming it behind him.

Chapter Six

The door banged shut. Tessa jumped, and fear prickled up her spine. Matt rarely got this angry. What would he do now? Take a walk to cool off or climb in the car and go for a long drive?

She paced to the front window and shoved aside the dusty curtain. Matt strode down the driveway but slowed as a black BMW rolled to a stop beside him. The window lowered, and Mallory Willard looked out.

The sudden smile on Matt's face jolted Tessa. She gripped the curtain and stared at their animated expressions. *Oh, Matt, don't make a fool of yourself with that woman.* Tessa balled her fists. Ooh! If only I could read their lips.

Mallory parked her car and climbed out. Matt continued talking to her and politely shut her door. She flashed him a smile and tossed her blond hair over her shoulder. She looked more like a fashion model than a lawyer in her slim black pants, bright red blouse, and black leather jacket.

Tessa straightened her shoulders, preparing to confront her. But rather than walking toward the lodge, they turned and headed down the secluded path toward the lake.

Tessa's eyes bulged, and her heart began to pound. Why

would Matt take a walk with that—that woman? The answer about slapped her in the face. Of course he wouldn't want to bring Mallory back to the lodge after the way Tessa had been acting.

Regret cooled her anger. Perhaps she should have at least looked at his business proposal. But how could she even consider moving here? His plan would plunge their family back into debt and destroy her sagging sense of security. She'd have to give up her business and move far away from her family and friends. She'd lose daily contact with her sister. And with all Allison was going through, she needed Tessa.

But what about Matt? Shouldn't her first commitment be to her husband?

Tessa sighed and closed her eyes as her confused thoughts tumbled through her mind. She didn't want to give up her life in Princeton for the frightening risks of Matt's far-fetched scheme. Why couldn't he settle down and be happy in New Jersey where everything was safe and predictable? Why couldn't he understand her needs and desires?

* * * *

Matt pulled in a deep breath of cool mountain air. There was nothing like the refreshing scent of Douglas fir and the pungent aroma of the damp, mossy forest floor. Being here made him feel alive. These woods were nothing like the steel and glass cityscape he viewed from his third-floor office window.

"Matt?"

"Sorry." He glanced at Mallory. "Guess I was daydreaming."

"That's okay. This place inspires me to do a little dreaming myself." She gazed up at the huge fir trees along the path leading back to the lodge. "Do you know how lucky you are to inherit a piece of property like this?"

He nodded and then frowned slightly, realizing once again the awesome responsibility his uncle's gift had placed on his shoulders. Would he be able to develop the land in a way that preserved and protected the forest, or would he be forced to sell it to someone who wouldn't care about its natural beauty?

"I'm sorry I forgot that list of contractors," Mallory said. "Would you like me to give you a call when I get back to the office?" They stepped from the shade of the forest path and crunched across the gravel driveway toward Mallory's car.

Matt glanced toward the lodge. "Sure. That would be fine." The memory of Tessa's angry words rose and squelched the delight he had felt only moments before. He was too embarrassed to tell Mallory that he and Tessa couldn't agree about the future of his uncle's property.

"Anything else you need, just give me a call." Her gaze lingered, and he noticed her eyes were the same deep blue as Lost Lake.

"Dad! Look what we found!" Evan rushed toward him, carrying a rusty coffee can. "Justin said it's a saladmander."

Justin laughed and shook his head as he and Brie followed Evan out of the forest. "That's salamander, Ev."

Matt leaned down to take a look at the squiggly black creature swimming in the slimy-looking lake water. "Well, look at that."

"Isn't he cool?" Evan grinned with delight. "I never saw one of these before except on the Nature Channel. His back is really smooth. You want to touch him?" Evan held the can out toward Matt and Mallory.

She shook her head and melted back against the car. "No, no thanks."

"He won't hurt you." Evan lifted the can a little higher.

Matt held back a chuckle. "I think that's close enough, Evan." Mallory might appreciate the beauty of the forest, but she obviously wasn't too fond of the creatures inhabiting the lake.

Brie sent her dad a knowing glance. "Come on, Evan. Let's take him back to the house and show Mom."

Evan's eyes lit up at this new possibility, and he streaked off toward the lodge, lake water sloshing out of his can.

Matt studied Mallory as she brushed a tiny drop of water from the sleeve of her leather jacket. In spite of the perturbed pucker of her lips, she was a very attractive woman. But her chin had a haughty tilt, and he'd noticed an edge in her voice when she spoke to the kids, hinting at another person behind the smile.

"You certainly have your hands full with these kids." She looked up and caught him watching her. She smiled. "But I like the way you handle them."

"They keep me on my toes." He watched his kids scale the front steps, each one unique and so special. He'd do just about anything to make them happy and be sure their future was secure.

Mallory climbed into her car and closed her door. Lowering the window, she smiled at him once more. "Call me. Anytime. I want to do whatever I can to help you. It's a wonderful plan, and I can tell you're just the man who can pull it off."

A warm rush of pleasure shot through him as he replayed Mallory's flattering words, but it faded away as he watched her drive off.

He turned and trudged back toward the lodge. He dreaded facing his wife. Why had he stormed off like that? He rarely walked out on an argument, and he never slammed doors. As he considered what to do next, he could almost hear what his friend Keith would say. "You blew it, Matt. You need to go back in there and apologize. You'll never win Tessa over by bulldozing her. "

Matt rubbed his forehead. *Lord, I haven't been handling this very well. You know how much I want to make this move. I think it would be best for all of us. Please soften Tessa's heart, and help me trust You to work this out.*

Matt pulled open the screen door and walked into the living room.

"Evan, would you please put that salamander outside?" Tessa straightened up from tying twine around a large stack of old newspapers. "Then go up and change into a clean pair of jeans. You're all muddy." She shot a glance at Matt and then averted her eyes.

"Aw, Mom, can't I keep him in here?"

"Listen to your mother, Evan." Matt crossed the room toward them. "He'll be fine on the porch for now. After lunch, I think we should take him back down to the lake and let him go."

"But, Dad, I want to keep him for a pet."

"Think about that, buddy. There's not much food for him in that can. You wouldn't want him to starve, would you?"

Evan's eyes widened. "No, I guess not."

"Take him outside, and then run up and change." Matt gave his son a playful swat on the seat of his pants. Evan scampered out to the porch. He shot back past them and dashed up the stairs.

Matt watched Tessa kneel down to tie another stack of newspapers. Her faded blue jeans and a loose red shirt couldn't hide her attractive, petite figure. Even at forty-seven she still looked great to him. She had replaced her usual dangly earrings with little gold posts, and she'd tucked her short dark brown hair behind her ears while she worked. It reminded him of the way she looked that first day they met.

His heart twisted. "Listen, Tessa. I shouldn't have walked out like that. I'm sorry."

She focused on tying the twine into a tight knot.

He squatted down next to her. "I know I haven't really heard what you have to say about moving here, so . . . I'm ready to listen."

Her hand froze, and she slowly lifted her gaze to meet his. The suspicion in her eyes cut him to the heart. Would he ever win back her trust?

"I don't want to move here, Matt. I want to stay in Princeton." Her voice trembled.

He nodded and waited for her to say more, but she silently blinked back tears and looked away.

"Okay. I hear you, and I'm not going to force you into this. But I think we both need some more time and information before we make a final decision. How about I call a Realtor or two and have them come out and do a market analysis? We can ask some questions and find out what we would need to do to put it on the market."

Tessa sat back on her heels and looked at him doubtfully.

"I'd also like to have a contractor come out and look at

the lodge and cabins and give us some estimates on renovations. Then I'd like us to sit down and talk things over. We don't have to make a decision this week, but I think we should look at all the possibilities while we're here, including my business proposal."

Tessa pressed her lips together. "Okay. I suppose that's fair."

"Then there's one more thing I'd like us to do."

"What?"

"I'd like us to pray about this—together."

A wary look returned to Tessa's eyes. She stood and folded her arms across her chest.

He knew his request surprised her. They didn't have a habit of praying together. The last time they had prayed as a couple was when his father faced a serious heart surgery more than two years ago.

She released a soft sigh. "All right."

Chapter Seven

Tessa wrapped her hands around her teacup and let the warmth flow into her fingers. Settling back in the chair, she took a sip and stared out Sweet Something's rain-drizzled front windows. Cars buzzed down Princeton's historic Nassau Street, but the rain had kept all but a few hardy customers away.

She lowered her gaze to the wholesale grocery order form on the table in front of her and squinted at the tiny print. It would be impossible for her to fill it out without going back to the kitchen for her glasses.

Growing older could be such a pain. But it wasn't only blurred vision that bothered her. The decision hanging over her head left her feeling anxious and unsettled. They'd returned from Oregon three days ago, but she and Matt still couldn't agree on the future of Lost Lake Lodge. Oh, she'd looked over his business proposal. And they'd received bids from two contractors for renovations, but the money required to move ahead on either of those options had shocked her into angry silence.

Praying with Matt only made her feel more pressured. And now the kids were getting excited about the possibility of moving—even Brie! Tessa couldn't believe the way her daughter had turned traitor and sided with Matt as soon as her boyfriend, Ryan, began discussing attending Oregon State University.

Tessa rubbed her forehead. How would they ever be able to send any of their kids away to college if their finances became tangled up in that crazy lodge project?

The bell over the front door jingled. Bill Hancock stepped inside and glanced around. He smiled and waved when he saw Tessa. He wore charcoal slacks and a soft-gray V-neck sweater over a light blue shirt that matched the color of his eyes. Threads of silver in his dark hair and deep creases created by his smile, added to his good looks.

"Welcome back." He laid his hand on the back of the chair opposite hers, obviously waiting for an invitation to sit down.

"Can I get you something?" she asked, rising from her chair. "I just took some blueberry scones out of the oven a few minutes ago."

"Sounds great." He winked, and his smile deepened.

She blushed and silently scolded herself. Bill was just a friend—though his compliments and lingering looks suggested he might like to be more if circumstances were different. But he'd never done anything more than flirt, and she'd never done anything except enjoy his attention; still, a small cloud of guilt shadowed her heart. "Would you like coffee?"

"Yes, thanks." He took a seat, and she felt his gaze follow her as she turned and walked away.

When she stepped into the kitchen, her sister Allison met her. "More customers?"

"Just Bill Hancock. I'll take care of him."

A fleeting frown crossed Allison's face. "Don't let him

140

monopolize your afternoon."

Tessa heard the subtle warning behind her sister's words. She turned away and poured Bill's coffee into a mug. "I can't very well ignore him. He's a good customer and a fellow business owner." She chose the largest scone on the cooling rack and put it on a plate.

"I know, but I don't trust him."

"Why would you say that? He's always been friendly to me."

"That's exactly what I mean." Allison lifted her brows and sent Tessa a serious look. "Just be careful."

"Don't worry." She scooped up the tray and strolled out of the kitchen. Sometimes her sister could be such a wet blanket. There was nothing wrong with talking to Bill. His visits made her forget about her troubles. And for a little while each afternoon, he made her feel young and attractive again. What was wrong with that?

"Wow, that looks delicious." Bill smiled as she set the scone and coffee on the table in front of him.

Tessa glanced at her half-full teacup.

"I didn't mean to cut your break short," Bill said. "You've probably been on your feet all day. Please, sit down."

Something melted inside her at his thoughtfulness, and she took a seat. "Thanks. I am feeling a little tired. Jet lag, I guess."

"How was your trip?" He poured cream into his coffee.

Conflicting emotions swirled through her. "Oregon is beautiful. I've never seen huge mountains and evergreen forests like that." She hesitated and looked into Bill's eyes. "My husband wants us to move there."

"You're kidding." Bill frowned and laid aside his spoon.

"My husband's uncle left him an old mountain lodge

with seven guest cabins. Matt thinks we should renovate the property and rent out the cabins. But we'd have to take out a huge loan or find investors to pay for it." She clucked her tongue, and disgust crept into her voice. "I don't understand how he can even consider it. I'd have to pull the kids out of school, and we'd be all the way across the country from my family. And who knows how long it would be before we'd make an income from the cabins." She shivered at that frightening thought.

"What about Sweet Something?"

Her throat tightened. "I'd have to give it up." She glanced around the teashop and remembered how she and Allison had hunted all over Pennsylvania and New Jersey to find just the right antiques to give Sweet Something a special look. They'd tested recipes and developed the menu, stocked the gift shop, and worked long hours to build their business. What would happen if she pulled out and left Allison to manage it on her own? The teashop was important to her sister, but spending time with her husband and creating paintings for her limited-edition print collection took time, too.

"Is the decision final?"

"No, but Matt's pretty determined to go."

Bill's blue eyes took on a frosty glint. "Don't let him push you into doing something you'll regret."

"What choice do I have? If he says we're going, it's settled." She crossed her arms and tried to swallow the angry lump in her throat.

Bill pulled back and looked at her curiously. "Wait a minute. Why should he be the one to make that decision? What you want is important, too. You've worked hard to make your business successful." He pressed his lips together in a firm line. "Don't let him force you into giving up your shop."

An uncomfortable shiver passed through her. "Well, he's not really forcing me. He thinks it would be a good move for the whole family, and running his own business has been his dream for a long time."

"If that's what he wants, maybe you should let him go for it. But that doesn't mean you have to go, too."

Surprise rippled through her.

"People's goals and desires change. Sometimes everyone is happier if they follow their own path and pursue their own dreams."

She'd never considered the possibility of staying in Princeton while Matt worked in Oregon. Didn't some couples live in different cities and commute to see each other on weekends or vacations? But what kind of marriage would that be? How would an arrangement like that affect their children? Doubt swirled through her.

"This is an important decision, Tessa. There's a lot at stake."

Bill rested both arms on the table and leaned toward her. "Don't make the mistake of throwing away your dreams."

* * * *

Matt stuffed his hands into his jacket pockets as he crossed the park toward the Little League baseball diamond. Birds sang in the maple trees, and the air had a fresh rain-washed scent. If only he had different news to tell Tessa. But maybe this was best. At least the decision was out of their hands.

He focused on the small crowd seated on the metal

bleachers and soon spotted Tessa and Brie in the third row. Justin stood by the dugout, his black baseball cap pulled low over his eyes as he watched his little brother's game. Matt smiled as his gaze settled on Evan standing behind third base. His son leaned forward, ready for the next play.

Matt greeted a few parents and then climbed the bleachers. Tessa scooted over and made room for him. He settled on the bench next to her. "How's Evan doing?"

"He's played three of the five innings, walked once, and struck out twice."

Matt nodded, watching Tessa, trying to guess her mood. It had been a rocky week. His patience had been strained to the max as pressure increased at work and Tessa remained set against moving. If he hadn't had Keith's support, he didn't know how he would've made it. His friend's advice ran through his mind again. "Love her. Listen to her concerns. Wait for the Lord to bring her around. Don't push it."

He blew out a deep breath. What would Keith say now? Today's events had changed everything. He cleared his throat. "Brie, is the concession stand open?"

She leaned forward and looked around Tessa. "Yeah, why?"

"Would you get us some sodas?"

Brie cocked her head. "You feeling okay, Dad?"

He grimaced and reached for his wallet. "I'm fine." She didn't need to remind him that one trip to the concession stand could wipe out their entertainment budget for the week. They usually brought drinks and snacks from home to save money. Well, those days were almost over. He handed his daughter a ten, and she climbed down the bleachers.

"What was that about?" Tessa watched him curiously.

"We need to talk, and I thought it would be better to do it without an audience."

Apprehension creased her forehead. "What is it?"

"Madden sold out. My job's been cut."

Tessa gasped. "They fired you?"

"No, they eliminated my position. But don't worry; they gave me a severance package."

"What are we going to do? The money I make from Sweet Something will barely cover our rent. How will we pay for utilities or food? And what about the car payments?"

He glanced around, hoping no one had overheard her frantic questions. "Calm down, Tessa. It's not like we're going to be homeless next week. The severance package should cover our expenses for at least three months. The kids can finish the school year, and then it will pay for our moving expenses and help us get started with the renovations."

His wife's face paled. "What are you saying?"

He took her hands. "We asked the Lord to show us if we should move. I'd say this makes it pretty clear."

She stiffened and pulled back. "Just because you lost your job, that doesn't mean we have to move. You can look for another job, here in Princeton."

"Tessa, you know how tight the job market is here."

"But you have experience and connections. Surely you can find something."

"Why should I look here when we own Lost Lake Lodge? We can develop a great family business there and live the kind of life most people only dream about. I'm not talking so much about a big income. I think that's going to happen eventually, but I mean being a closer, stronger family."

Tessa's hands trembled in his, and fear darkened her

eyes. If only he could infuse her heart with more faith— faith in him and in God. But she had to make that choice herself. All he could do was tell her the truth and pray she would understand.

"I believe God's leading us to move to Oregon. I think this will be good for all of us." He gripped her hands more tightly, feeling like he stood balanced on the edge of a huge cliff. "I need you, Tessa. Come with me, be my partner, help me make this plan work."

Tears pooled in her dark eyes. "It doesn't make sense to me, Matt. We'd be giving up so much. How can I say yes?" She pulled her icy hands away and lifted her chin. "You go ahead and chase your dream. The kids and I aren't going anywhere."

Her words slammed into him like a Mack truck doing seventy, and he felt himself fall over the edge of the cliff.

Chapter Eight

Matt tucked a heavy green sweatshirt into his suit-case next to his hiking boots. Though it was almost Memorial Day, the temperatures would probably still be cool in the Cascades. He reached for his Bible on the night-stand, but his hand hesitated over the family photo taken last Christmas. The kids' smiling faces shone back at him, hope and mischief lighting their eyes.

He ran his finger along the top of the frame and lifted it for a closer look. A shard of pain twisted through him. He'd never been away from them for more than a week. How long would it be this time?

His gaze moved to his wife's pensive face. Even in this Christmas photo, apprehension clouded her expression. He'd tried everything he could think of to convince her to go to Oregon with him. But she wouldn't budge. She didn't believe he had what it took to make the lodge project suc-cessful. Bottom line: She didn't trust him.

Maybe his pride and self-sufficiency were leading him toward a dead end. But what other choice did he have? He couldn't just sit here in New Jersey and do nothing. He needed to bring in an income, and getting the guest cabins ready to rent this summer was a start. He studied the photo a moment longer, then carefully wrapped it in a T-shirt and laid it in the suitcase along with his Bible.

"Hey, Dad." Justin leaned in the doorway. "What time is your plane tomorrow?"

Heaviness settled over Matt. "I'm leaving around five thirty in the morning."

Justin nodded and stuffed his hands into his jeans pockets. He glanced at the suitcase and back at his dad. "I want to come out there as soon as finals are over."

Matt's heart warmed. "I could use your help, but I thought you planned to work full-time for Pete this summer." Matt knew his son's hours at the construction company increased with warmer weather, and that would provide the money he needed for college classes next fall.

"If I give my notice now, I could come by mid-June."

Matt walked over and laid his hand on his son's shoulder. "It would be great to have you there with me, but I don't want to make you miss a semester."

"It's okay, Dad. I'm not talking about quitting college. I just want to take some time off to help you out."

Matt's throat tightened, and he squeezed Justin's shoulder. "I appreciate that, but your mom wants you to stay on track so you can transfer to a university in another year."

"It wouldn't hurt to take a semester off. Once we get the cabins cleaned up and rented out, we'll make enough money to pay for school. And if I go with you this summer, I can establish residency and apply to schools in Oregon."

For a moment Matt could see it all happening. He and Justin would work together over the summer, building a closer relationship as they fixed up the cabins and restored the old lodge to its former beauty. Tessa, Brie, and Evan would join them after school was out, and the whole family would be together. But reality quickly washed over him. Tessa would never agree to it. She'd already signed Evan up for summer day camp. Brie had a part-time job lined up at the mall. Tessa wouldn't hear of Matt disrupting the children's summer plans. If he forced the issue, it would only hurt their relationship more. She left him no choice. He was going alone.

Sorrow shrouded Matt's heart as he looked into his son's eyes. "I'm sorry, Justin, I think you need to stay here, hold on to your job, and stick to the plan we made with Mom."

"But, Dad—"

Brie and Evan marched into the room. "We want to go, too," Brie insisted.

Evan stepped in front of his sister. "Yeah. Why should I have to go to day camp when I could be in the real woods with you?"

Matt suppressed a proud grin. "You two sound pretty serious about this."

"We are!" Brie's dark eyes flashed. "All of us staying here while you go to Oregon is a bad idea. Come on, Dad. This is never going to work."

How could he convince them to accept a plan he didn't feel was best? But for Tessa's sake he had to squelch this mutiny. He motioned them all closer. "Look, this is a really tough time for all of us. Neither your mom nor I are happy about this decision, but it's the best we can come up with right now." His gaze moved around the semicircle of gloomy faces. "So while I'm gone, I want you guys to cooperate with Mom and help her out. She's going to need you." Matt's voice grew thick as he thought of leaving Tessa and the kids on their own.

Out of the corner of his eye, he caught a movement

and looked up. Tessa hesitated in the doorway. A painful expression crossed her face.

Matt straightened and focused on the kids. "Why don't you guys head on out. I'll come around and say good night in a little while."

With tired sighs and sagging shoulders, the kids filed out the bedroom door.

Matt focused on his suitcase and rearranged a few pairs of rolled-up socks.

"They blame me for everything." Tessa's voice vibrated with emotion. "It's not fair. This is just as much your decision as it is mine."

Matt closed his eyes, reining in his temper. He would not argue with Tessa. This was their last night together for who knew how long.

"Did you pack some warm clothes?" Her voice softened.

"I'll be fine." Matt pulled another turtleneck from the drawer and folded it into the suitcase. He heard Tessa cross the room. His heart hammered. Did she finally realize how much her painful choices were costing their family?

"You don't have to do this, Matt. It's not too late to change your mind."

His hopes crashed, and his heart hardened. He slowly turned and faced her. "The door swings both ways, Tessa."

Her stony expression faltered, and tears glistened in her eyes, but she turned and walked away.

* * * *

Tessa lay in bed, still as a stone, pretending to be asleep. She peeked out from under the comforter. Matt lugged his suitcase toward the bedroom door. He slowed for a moment, his bulky silhouette outlined in the soft glow from the night-light in the hall. She closed her eyes so he wouldn't guess she was awake. Saying good-bye again would only hurt more.

The door closed with a soft click. Darkness enveloped the room. Tessa heard the suitcase wheels roll down the hallway. Hot, silent tears coursed down her cheeks. She didn't think he'd really leave. But it was happening. And somehow she felt like the nightmare had only begun.

* * * *

"Bring me more towels!" Panic rushed through Tessa as she tried to hold back the rising water with the pile of sopping towels.

She'd sent her daughter next door to get their elderly neighbor, Walter Cooper. Hopefully he would know how to stop the torrent gushing from the broken cold-water handle in the shower.

For the hundredth time, she moaned and berated herself for sending her husband off to Oregon. What kind of fool was she? Handling life on her own had been nothing short of a disaster.

On Tuesday the dryer broke, and the repairman couldn't come until next week. On Wednesday her key jammed in the ignition, and she had to have the van towed to the dealer. Last night Justin had stayed out past his curfew—again. When she confronted him, he glared at her and insisted he shouldn't have to stick to the same schedule he'd kept, since his classes at the community college were finished. That same day, Brie broke up with her boyfriend, Ryan, and was inconsolable. Then just before dinner, Evan's teacher called and said she was concerned about his moodiness and poor performance over the last two weeks—exactly the length of time Matt had been gone. And now this plumbing catastrophe!

"Brie! Where are you?" Tessa gritted her teeth and tried to shove the sloppy wave back toward the shower stall, but it gushed over the top of her towel barrier and surged toward the door. Tears flooded her eyes like the mini tidal wave in her bathroom. If only Matt were here. He'd know what to do. He was so good with the kids, and he could fix anything.

The doorbell chimed. Tessa groaned, turned away from the mess, and headed downstairs. Glancing in the mirror on the wall of the entryway, she skidded to a stop. Tears still shimmered in her eyes, mascara smudged her cheeks, and her wet clothes clung to her. Well, there was nothing she could do about it now. She pulled open the door and froze.

Bill Hancock stood on the porch holding a large arrangement of bright spring flowers. His eyes widened. "Tessa? What happened?"

Embarrassment zinged through her like an electric shock. "My—my daughter was taking a shower, and the handle broke off. I've got a flood upstairs, and I have no idea how to shut it off."

"Would you like me to come in and take a look?"

Relief washed over her. "Oh, would you?"

"Sure, show me the way." He set the flowers on a nearby table. "These are for you. You've been so down in the dumps, I was hoping they'd cheer you up."

She bit her lip, torn by his kindness and a feeling of guilt. "Thanks, Bill."

Within two minutes, Bill turned off the water to the entire house. Then he followed Tessa upstairs and insisted on helping her clean up the mess. Brie finally arrived with Mr. Cooper. She'd caught him napping in front of the TV and waited for him to put on his shoes and collect his tools before he came to help. Tessa thanked her neighbor and sent him home. She introduced Brie and Bill and then gave her daughter a pile of wet towels to tote to the laundry room. When Brie returned, she stood in the doorway and glared suspiciously at Bill.

Tessa forced a smile. "Thanks, Brie. I think we're about finished here."

Her daughter lifted her eyebrows, silently asking, who is this guy, and what's he doing here?

Ignoring her daughter's look, she turned to Bill. "Good thing you stopped by. We'd have drowned without your help."

He grinned. "Glad I decided to deliver those flowers myself."

"Flowers?" Brie's gaze darted from Bill to Tessa.

"Yes, Bill brought us a lovely bouquet to cheer us up. He had no idea we needed a plumber."

He chuckled. "Well, it doesn't take too much talent to push a mop around."

Brie rolled her eyes and flounced off down the hall.

Tessa swallowed her embarrassment and turned to Bill. "I do appreciate your help. And thanks again for the flowers. You didn't have to do that."

"Well, I admit I have another motive for my visit." He grinned and leaned against the doorjamb. "I have two tickets for the Princeton Medical Center gala dinner next Saturday, and I wondered if you'd like to go."

Tessa's breath caught in her throat. "I don't know, Bill."

"It would be a great way to make connections for Sweet Something. You'd be networking with Princeton's finest." When she hesitated, he sent her an understanding look. "You don't have to decide right now. Check your schedule. See if you can work it out."

She struggled to focus her spinning thoughts. Was he trying to help her business, or was he asking her out on a date? She looked into Bill's eyes, and something there hinted this invitation was more than a friendly business offer.

"No pressure. Just think about it, okay?"

She couldn't decide tonight. She needed more time. "Okay," she said softly. But as soon as she answered, doubt tossed her emotions back and forth like a choppy sea.

Chapter Nine

Matt strapped his leather tool belt around his waist and leaned the extension ladder against the side of cabin number four. Once he fixed the roof, this cabin would be ready for rental. A warm sense of satisfaction flowed through him as he climbed to the top and glanced at the other three classic 1920s log cabins he had repaired over the last two weeks. Each one slept six and had a river-rock fireplace and full-length plank porch. He still had three more cabins to refurbish, but he could begin taking reservations anytime.

He pulled in a deep breath of fresh, evergreen-scented air and listened to the wind in the fir trees. The quiet had been hard to get used to at first, especially after living in a busy family of five. Though he'd grown accustomed to his peaceful surroundings, he missed his family and the comfort of the relationships and routines they shared every day.

His only contact with home was his nightly phone call. Sometimes that hurt so much he could hardly force himself to dial the number. The kids poured out their stories, making him ache to be there, but Tessa always kept her conversation brief and businesslike. She never even hinted at missing him or changing her mind about coming to Oregon. His heart hurt every time he thought of all that separated them—not just physical distance, but broken dreams and shattered trust.

He heard a car approaching and leaned to the left to check it out. A black BMW pulled in and parked. The car door opened, and Mallory Willard stepped out. Matt's stomach tensed. This was her fourth visit since he'd returned to work on renovations. He was beginning to think she had more than legal work on her mind.

Long blond hair shimmered in the sunlight as it fell over her shoulders, and her black pants and blue sweater showed off her great figure. Heat flashed up his neck, and he shifted his focus. Maybe if he didn't say anything, she'd think he wasn't home and leave. He huffed out a disgusted breath. What kind of coward was he? He could handle Mallory Willard.

"Hey, Mallory, I'm up here." He waved.

She looked up and sent him a dazzling smile. "Well, aren't you the brave one. What are you doing way up there?"

"Just working on the roof." He climbed down and walked over to meet her.

"Everything looks wonderful. I can't believe all you've accomplished in just two weeks."

"Thanks." He let his gaze travel around the property. She was right. It looked like a different place. Earlier this week, he'd hired a couple men to clear out the weeds, trim the bushes, and begin some basic landscaping.

"I hope you're hungry." She reached back into her car and pulled out a large wicker basket.

A warning flashed through him. "What's that?"

"Barbecued chicken, roasted vegetables, potato salad, and the best strawberry pie you've ever tasted."

"Wow, I was going to eat leftover pizza."

"You deserve much more than that after all this hard work."

Her inviting smile and tempting menu made Matt's head swim. Why not invite her in and enjoy the food she'd made? But what would Tessa say if she found out? How would he explain having dinner, alone, with an attractive woman like Mallory Willard?

"Let's go inside." She smiled and dangled the basket in front of him.

The scent of barbecued chicken drifted out, making his mouth water. "I guess I can take a break for a few minutes." He led her to the lodge, fighting a battle with his conscience. *She is offering more than a home-cooked meal, and you know it. It's okay; I'll just eat the food and get right back to work.*

Mallory stepped inside and set the basket on the coffee table. "Why don't you go clean up while I get things ready?" Matt glanced down at his dirty shirt and hands. "Sure. I'll . . . uh, be right back." He took the stairs two at a time and pulled off his shirt as he hustled down the upstairs hall. After snatching a clean shirt from his closet, he headed for the bathroom. The warm water felt good as he ran it over his hands. Leaning forward, he splashed his face, grabbed a towel, and looked up at the mirror.

Staring at his dripping reflection, a powerful wave of conviction broke over him. He closed his eyes and sighed heavily. Nothing would wash away his guilt if he didn't go downstairs right now and put an end to this. No matter how hungry or lonely he felt, he loved the Lord and his family too much to put himself in a tempting situation with Mallory Willard.

He tossed the towel on the counter and walked out of the bathroom. Verses he'd read in Proverbs that morning came back to him. He couldn't quote them perfectly, but he knew they said he'd pay a high price if he broke his marriage vows and got involved with another woman. The vivid word picture flashed in his mind—"Her lips drip honey, but in the end her feet go down to death. "

All right. I hear You, Lord.

When he reached the bottom step, he saw her standing by the roll top desk with the phone to her ear.

"No, he's busy," she said softly. "He can't come to the phone right now."

Matt frowned. Who was she talking to? "Mallory."

She spun around and quickly replaced the receiver. Her lips curved into an unconvincing smile. "Well, don't you clean up nicely."

"Who was that?"

She averted her eyes. "Just a wrong number."

She was lying. The call had probably been from one of his kids or, worse yet, from Tessa. Irritation coursed through him, confirming his decision. "Mallory, you need to leave."

"Why? What's the matter?" She crossed the room to meet him.

"I'm committed to my marriage, and inviting you in is sending you the wrong message."

Her eyes widened with false innocence. "But we haven't done anything wrong."

"Exactly. And I want to keep it that way." He strode to the door and pulled it open.

She huffed out a scornful laugh. "My, my, aren't you the noble one."

He hesitated, struggling with the truth, then looked her in the eye. "No, but I've made a commitment to God and to my wife, and I don't want to do anything that would hurt my family or damage the name of Christ." A rush of victory flooded him, and he held the door open wider. "Good-bye, Mallory." She lifted her chin, and her electric blue eyes flashed. "You're throwing away the possibility of a great relationship. Is that what you really want?"

Doubt tugged at his resolve for a second. He needed a miracle to win back Tessa's love, but this was no time to give up on his marriage or do something stupid. He raised his gaze and met hers. "I made up my mind twenty-five years ago when I married Tessa. Nothing is going to change that."

Flames singed her cheeks, and her lips twitched. "Then you're a bigger fool than I thought." She snatched the basket off the coffee table, leaving the food behind as she strutted out the door. Two seconds later, he heard her car door slam and the spray of gravel as she sped down the driveway and out of his life.

He leaned back against the door and closed his eyes. "Thank You," he whispered. Then he headed down the path to the lake to continue his conversation with the Lord.

* * * *

Tessa carried the last three bags of groceries into the house, dreading the mess she knew awaited her in the kitchen.

Her selfish complaints about Matt's lack of help taunted

her. Since he left she felt like she swam through a soupy sea, barely able to keep her head above water. She'd never realized or appreciated all he did. Now there was no one to share the load. Tonight she had to find some way to dry two loads of laundry, help Evan with his math, and pick up Brie from work, but first she had to put away all these groceries.

Evan looked at her with a perplexed expression as she came in the door. "Something weird is going on."

She sighed and lowered the heavy bags to the floor. "What do you mean, honey?"

"I just called Dad, and some woman answered and said he was busy and couldn't come to the phone."

A chill raced up Tessa's back. "You probably dialed the wrong number. Try again."

Evan shook his head. "I used your phone 'cause the number's programmed in."

Tessa swallowed and clasped her hands in front of her to hide their trembling. *Oh, Father, what's happening? Have I pushed him away—right into the arms of another woman?* The image of the tall, blond lawyer rose in her mind, and her stomach clenched. That woman's interest in Matt had been obvious from the first day they arrived. Had she been chasing Matt while Tessa selfishly ignored his pleas to bring the kids and come to Oregon?

Was he fighting a battle for their marriage, or had he already given up and given in? "Hand me the phone, Evan."

"You okay, Mom?"

She nodded, trying to swallow her rising fear. "I'm fine. Why don't you put away some groceries for me."

Evan quietly pulled a box of cereal from the closest bag and watched her punch in the number. She ought to take the conversation into another room, but her feet felt glued to the floor. Matt's phone rang. Tessa held her breath. What would she say if that woman answered? After three more rings, the answering machine picked up. Her heart twisted at the sound of his voice. Why didn't he answer? What were they doing?

She cleared her throat. "Matt, it's me. Please call. We need to talk." She could hardly choke out the last sentence. Evan stared at her and then walked out of the kitchen, his shoulders slumping. She heard him click on the TV in the living room.

She mechanically put away groceries, anxiety and regret weighing down every motion. How many times had she ignored her husband's needs and let her own fears and resentment build a wall between them? Had she destroyed her marriage with her own willful choices? But didn't Matt have some responsibility, too? Wasn't he the one who'd gone off to Oregon and left her here?

The truth hit her hard. She had chosen to hold on to her anger rather than forgive and believe the best in her husband. Her lack of trust in Matt, and ultimately in the Lord, was hurting them all. The weight of her sin and the cost it was extracting from her family felt like a crushing weight on her shoulders.

Father, help me! I'm so sorry. Please don't let it be too late.

Evan drifted back into the kitchen, a worried look in his eyes. "Don't you have to pick up Brie?"

Tessa checked the kitchen clock and snatched her keys off the counter. "Come on, we're already late."

Raindrops pelted the windshield as she backed the van out of the garage. Lightning split the sky, followed by a frightening boom of thunder. She flipped the wipers on high, trying to see through the sheets of rain. She hated driving in storms, but she couldn't leave her daughter stranded at the mall.

As Tessa merged onto the rain-slick highway, her stomach knotted and her thoughts spun into a tangled web. How had her life gotten so out of control? Had she become so absorbed with her problems that she'd drifted away from the Lord and closed her ears to His voice? The memory of Bill's dinner invitation sent a huge wave of guilt crashing over her. How could she have even considered it? The thunderstorm outside was nothing compared to the tempest in her heart.

Forgive me, Father. Please forgive me. Tears rained silently down her cheeks. She choked back a sob to hide her distress from her son, who sat behind her.

Red taillights flashed ahead. She slowed, but a pickup truck cut into her lane, trying to squeeze into the shrinking space between her and the next car. Tessa gasped, slammed on the brakes, and swerved to the left. A horn blared behind her. She frantically jerked the steering wheel to the right. Tires screeched, metal crunched, and Evan's scream pierced the night and tore her heart in two.

Chapter Ten

The phone rang as Matt walked in the door of the lodge. It had to be Tessa. He dashed across the room. Please, Lord, help me straighten this out. Would she let him explain, or would this be the final blow that broke their fragile bond? No, he'd just turned everything over to the Lord. He had to hold on to the hope he'd been given. He willed confidence into his voice as he answered.

"Oh, Matt." Tessa's voice shook.

He gripped the phone. "What's wrong?"

"I had an accident." Tears laced her words.

"Are you hurt?"

"No—no, I'm okay, just a little cut on my forehead." She sniffed, her voice still trembling. "But we were hit from behind, and Evan was . . ."

The floor seemed to drop out from under him, and he grabbed the desk chair. "Is he okay?"

"No, we're in the Princeton emergency room. They're taking him to surgery." Tessa broke into jerky sobs.

He closed his eyes and sank into the chair, groaning a heartfelt, wordless prayer.

"I'm so sorry, Matt." Grief choked her voice.

He shuddered and drew in a sharp breath. Was she

talking about the accident or the trouble between them? It didn't matter. He could never blame her for any of it. This was just as much his fault as hers. He should've been there to protect his family and prevent something tragic like this from happening.

Sorrow clogged his throat. He leaned forward and rubbed his burning eyes.

"Please come home, Matt. We need you."

Her words infused him with new strength, and he rose to his feet. "I'm already on the way." He heard more crying on her end of the line, making him long to be there and hold her.

"The Lord is going to carry us through this. Hold on to Him, Tessa."

"I will, but please hurry," she whispered.

* * * *

An elderly woman wearing a blue volunteer smock checked the hospital's computer and looked up with a smile. "Your son is in room 127. That's one floor up in Pediatrics on B-1."

Matt nodded and breathed a silent prayer of thanks as he strode toward the elevator. The news that Evan was in a regular room, not in surgery or intensive care, boosted his tired spirit. He followed the signs, rounded several corners, and passed the nurses' station. No one had answered the home phone or their cell phones, so Matt hoped he would find Tessa and the kids here.

His journey from Lost Lake Lodge to the University Medical Center of Princeton had taken only eleven hours and twenty-five minutes. He knew that was nothing short of a miracle since he'd had no reservation, and he'd managed to get one of the last seats available on the only plane flying from Portland to Philadelphia late last night. He'd flown off into the midnight sky and then watched the sun come up and fill the heavens with light, his prayers and hope rising with the dawn. Though the circumstances surrounding his return were serious, he felt an unexplained peace. The Lord was at work.

Matt spotted room 127, and his heart lurched. What if he had manufactured those feelings of hope and peace in his own imagination and they weren't from the Lord? What if they lost Evan?

No, he would not let doubt or fear creep in and steal what he had been given. The Lord would be with them no matter what happened.

The door stood slightly ajar. He whispered one more prayer and walked through. The sight of a sterile, empty bed shook him for a moment, but then he saw a curtain had been pulled to shield a second bed. He braced himself and stepped around the curtain.

His gaze darted from his sleeping son to his wife. She had pulled her chair up to Evan's bedside and sat as close to him as possible with her head resting near his, her eyes closed, her hand covering his small fingers.

Matt stalled, practically bowled over by a powerful wave of love for them. The tranquil looks on both their faces told him his prayers for their comfort had been answered. He took a deep breath, trying to collect his emotions.

Stepping closer, he leaned down and brushed a gentle kiss across Tessa's cheek. Her eyelashes fluttered, and recognition crossed her sleepy expression. She rose into his embrace. Neither spoke as they held each other tightly.

Tears washed his eyes, and he let them fall, unashamed. Oh, how he loved this woman.

"I'm so glad you're here," she finally whispered.

"Me, too." He sighed into her hair, holding her close. Right then, he made a decision. No matter what it took, he'd rebuild his marriage and show his wife and kids how much he loved them. With God's help he'd do it.

* * * *

Tessa clung to Matt, drinking in the comfort of his strong embrace. She pressed her cheek to his chest, and the soothing scent that was Matt's alone filled her senses. She finally pulled back and looked into his face, wanting to study each line and feature that was so familiar and dear to her.

"How's Evan?" He clasped her hand and glanced toward their son, concern filling his eyes.

"He has a broken leg, but the doctors say he's going to be okay. At first they thought he had a concussion, but they did a CAT scan and ruled that out. He had a three-hour surgery last night to put in pins and repair the fracture. They gave him some pain medication. I guess that's why he's still asleep."

Matt nodded, his serious gaze still fixed on Evan.

Tessa's throat tightened. How could she ever have doubted his love and commitment to her and the kids? She must have been deaf to the truth and blinded by her own foolishness.

He turned to her and tenderly brushed her bangs away from the cut on her forehead. "And how are you?"

Heat raced into her cheeks at his close scrutiny. Did

he see the crow's-feet, smudged makeup, and dark circles under her eyes? He smiled, and her fears vanished. His loving look convinced her he saw past all of that into her heart, and he treasured her.

A hot, exultant tear trickled down her cheek. "I love you, Matt. Can you forgive me for being so selfish and hurting you and the kids?"

He reached for her. "Only if you'll forgive me for trying to push you into something you never wanted. That was way out of line."

They spent the next half hour talking about the issues that had put a strain on their marriage and assuring each other how much they loved each other.

"I don't want anything to ever come between us again," he said.

She smiled, awed by his sincerity. "Okay, but you have to promise me one thing."

"What's that?"

"That we'll spend the next twenty-five years together."

Surprise and then understanding flickered across his face. "Today's June sixteenth."

She grinned. "Happy anniversary."

"Wow, twenty-five years." Affection and longing glowed in his eyes. He lowered his head and kissed her, gently at first and then more deeply.

She wrapped her arms around his neck and returned his kiss, wanting to show him he was her first and only love. She didn't care what she had to leave behind. Nothing on earth meant as much to her as this dear, wonderful man and their life together. She'd made a commitment to him and him alone. Everything else needed to take a number and get in line.

Justin swished back the curtain and almost spilled the cardboard tray of fast food in his hands. "Dad!"

Brie rushed to hug her father. "Oh, Daddy!" The delight on their daughter's face gave her a glow Tessa hadn't seen for weeks.

Matt hugged Brie and then turned to Justin. "Come here, big guy." He opened his arms and welcomed his older son with a slap on the back and bear hug.

"Hey, what's going on?" a faint voice asked.

Tessa spun toward the bed.

Evan's dazed expression turned to one of pure joy. "Dad, you're here!"

Matt leaned down and gently embraced his tearful son. "Hey, sport. I'm sure glad to hear your voice. How are you doing?"

"I'm okay. When did you get here? How long are you staying? I want to go back with you." Evan's words tumbled out in a rush, and his chin quivered.

"Hey, slow down. It's okay; we've got plenty of time to talk about that."

Tessa pulled in a deep breath. "No, I think it's time for a family meeting."

They all looked at her, surprise on their faces.

Matt straightened. "You want to call a family meeting right now?"

"Yes. I have some things I need to say to all of you." She turned to Evan. "That is, if you're awake enough to listen."

He blinked his droopy eyes. "Sure, I broke my leg, but my ears are fine."

They all grinned.

"First, I need to apologize—to all of you." Tessa looked into each face. "When your dad and I talked and prayed about going to Oregon, we asked the Lord to make it clear if we should move. He did, but I didn't want to listen. I let selfishness and fear get in the way and make the decision for me, and that hurt us all. I need to trust the Lord to lead us, and we need a full-time dad and mom in this family, so—"

Matt interrupted her. "Wait. Before we make any decisions, I have some things to say, too. The Lord's also been speaking to me, and He's made it clear that keeping our family together is more important than where we live or work. And if that means I need to sell the lodge property and move home to New Jersey, then that's what I'll do. Living in Oregon would be a good choice for us, but it's not the only choice. I love you—all of you." He looked at each of them, and his gaze settled on Tessa. "And you're worth more to me than any piece of property, no matter how long it has been in my family or how much business potential it has."

Tessa smiled. "I love you, too, and I'm ready to move to Oregon if that's where you believe the Lord is leading us."

"But I could get a good price for that property. We could buy a new house here, and you could keep Sweet Something."

"Since you guys can't make up your mind, I think we should vote on it," Justin said.

Tessa and Matt exchanged surprised glances.

"All those in favor of moving to Oregon raise your hand," Justin continued.

Every hand went up, including Tessa's. Laughter bubbled up from her heart. The Lord had made it clear again, and this time she would listen.

"Yes!" Justin pumped his fist in the air.

Brie squealed and grabbed her big brother for a hug. Evan's sleepy smile spread wider, delight brightening his eyes.

Matt pulled Tessa close. "Are you sure, Tessa? Is this what you really want?"

Assurance washed over her. "Yes, I want to be with you. Wherever you're going, I'm going, too." Then she kissed him again, lingering, savoring the sweetness of their love tested and refined by twenty-five years of marriage and renewed by a miracle of God's grace in their hearts.

THE END

About the Author: Carrie Turansky has loved reading since she first visited the library as a young child and checked out a tall stack of picture books. Her love for writing began when she penned her first novel at age twelve. She is now the award-winning author of thirteen inspirational novels and novellas. Carrie and her husband, Scott, who is a pastor, author, and speaker, have been married over thirty-five years and make their home in New Jersey. They often travel together on ministry trips and to visit their five adult children and four grandchildren. Carrie also leads women's ministry at her church. When she's not writing she enjoys arranging flowers, cooking healthy meals for family and friends, and walking around the lake near their home. Carrie loves to connect with reading friends through her website, www.carrieturansky.com, and through Facebook, Pinterest, and Twitter.

Carrie's most recent novels include:

The Governess of Highland Hall

The Daughter of Highland Hall (October 2014)

Snowflake Sweethearts

A Man To Trust

Seeking His Love

Surrendered Hearts

Along Came Love

Christmas Mail-Order Brides

Made in the USA
Middletown, DE
11 May 2020